Tears filled
Ross frown
it? What hav

'It's not you, Ross. It's me. I should never have let things reach this point.'

'How can you say that?' he exclaimed, trying to draw her into his arms.

'Please don't. I'm sorry, Ross...'

'For God's sake, Heather, stop it! Don't do this to yourself or to me.' He didn't try to touch her again but the pain in his voice was more than enough to gain her attention. Heather's heart ached afresh because it was all her fault that he was suffering.

'Don't push me away again, Heather. Talk to me. Tell me what that problem is and then maybe we can find a solution. I...I know this has something to do with Grace's father and I swear that I'll understand.'

Jennifer Taylor lives in the north-west of England with her husband Bill. She had been writing Mills & Boon® romances for some years, but when she discovered Medical Romances™, she was so captivated by these heart-warming stories that she set out to write them herself! When she is not writing or doing research for her latest book, Jennifer's hobbies include reading, travel, walking her dog and retail therapy (shopping!). Jennifer claims all that bending and stretching to reach the shelves is the best exercise possible.

Recent titles by the same author:

HOME BY CHRISTMAS
HIS BROTHER'S SON
LIFE SUPPORT
MORGAN'S SON

SAVING
DR COOPER

BY
JENNIFER TAYLOR

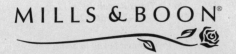

MILLS & BOON®

First published in Great Britain 2003
Harlequin Mills & Boon Limited,
Eton House, 18-24 Paradise Road, Richmond, Surrey TW9 1SR

© Jennifer Taylor 2003

ISBN 0 263 83449 2

Set in Times Roman 10 on 11 pt.
03-0603-61262

Printed and bound in Spain
by Litografia Rosés, S.A., Barcelona

CHAPTER ONE

THE call came in shortly before Red Watch were due to go off duty. Up till then the day had been unusually quiet. Weekends tended to be their busiest periods but there had been just one call that afternoon, to a fire started by some teenagers who'd set light to the contents of a skip left in the car park of a local supermarket.

It had taken the crew from Hexton fire station less than an hour to get the blaze under control and arrange for the skip to be collected. They'd been on their way back to the station when the second call had come through. It had been immediately apparent that this one wasn't going to be anywhere near as easy to deal with.

Ross Tanner nodded as one of the crew finished checking his breathing apparatus and gave him the thumbs-up sign. He waited impatiently while his colleague Terry Green's equipment was also checked. The fire had started in the basement flat of a run-down Victorian terrace and had spread rapidly through the four-storey building. Even from a distance of several hundred yards, the roar of the flames was deafening.

Crews from neighbouring fire stations had been called in to assist because of the danger that the fire would spread to the adjoining properties. That wasn't Ross's main concern, however. A three-year-old child had been reported as trapped inside the blazing building and the sooner they got him out the happier Ross would be.

'I don't want either of you taking risks. The upper floors could cave in at any moment. You're to get the hell out of there at the first sign of trouble.'

Ross listened while the senior divisional officer, Mike Rafferty—who was in charge of the fire ground—issued some last-minute instructions. As Station Officer at Hexton, Ross knew the rule, of course, that no firefighter should needlessly put his own life at risk. He also knew that when there was a child involved none of the men from Red Watch would hesitate. If there was a chance of saving the little boy then neither he nor his colleagues would pull out.

Ross led the way to the front of the blazing building and waited while the crew hosed him down. The equipment he was wearing was both heavy and cumbersome but he spent hours practising the drill each week and he was used to the weight of the air tank on his back and the difficulties of breathing through a mask. He was even used to the ferocity of the heat that greeted him as they entered the smoke-darkened hallway and made their way to the staircase at the rear.

He'd been a firefighter for ten years and he'd attended enough fires during that time to know what to expect. He was trained for this situation. He knew what to do. Now all he had to do was find the child and get him out…alive.

'Will I be glad when this shift is over. If I see one more person who's injured himself doing DIY then I swear I shall scream!'

Heather Cooper frowned as her colleague, Melanie Winters, laughed. 'What's so funny? Aren't you sick and tired of washing splinters out of eyes and sewing up cuts?'

'Oh, I am, I am.' Melanie grinned at her. 'It's just the thought of the oh-so-calm Dr Cooper letting rip which is so amusing. When have you ever lost your cool, Heather? You have to be the most *together* person I've ever met!'

'Hmm, appearances can be deceptive.'

Heather summoned a smile as she turned to the board to check which cubicles were still in use, but her soft grey eyes held more than a hint of pain.

None of the people she worked with could guess how hard it had been to get her life together in the last three years because she'd never discussed her past with any of them. It had been too difficult to talk about that terrible period in her life so she'd made the decision when she had accepted the job as senior registrar in the accident and emergency unit of St Gertrude's Hospital in south-east London not to tell anyone what had happened.

She picked up a duster and wiped the last patient's name from the board, feeling the tremor that coursed through her as the memory of those dark days came flooding back. After Stewart had died she'd come so close to giving up that at times it had been all she could do to get out of bed each morning. Even the fact that she'd been pregnant hadn't helped because all she'd been able to think about had been that she'd not had a chance to tell Stewart they'd been expecting a baby.

It had taken the birth of their daughter to give her the strength to carry on. Now Grace was her whole world and Heather wanted nothing more than to make sure that her precious little girl was safe and happy. Never again would she risk falling in love and leaving herself open to being hurt.

'Looks as though now might be a good time to take your break,' she suggested, turning to the younger woman with a smile that betrayed little of her true feelings. 'Why don't you go to the canteen and I'll go when you come back?'

'If you're sure…?' Melanie grinned when Heather nodded. 'Rightio, then. I did *just* happen to spot the gorgeous Dr Carlisle heading toward the lift. This could be the perfect opportunity to show him what's been missing from his life up till now, i.e. me!'

With a wave of her hand, the young nurse hurried away. Heather sighed. At twenty-three, Melanie was only ten years younger than she was, but at times it felt as though she was old enough to be Melanie's mother. Had she ever been that carefree? Would she ever feel that way again?

It took a determined effort to shake off the moment of introspection but Heather had become adept at controlling her emotions in the months since Grace's birth. Children picked up on mood swings so quickly and she refused to do anything that might upset the little girl. Far better to keep her feelings to herself than risk letting them affect her precious daughter.

She made her way to the end cubicle and pushed back the

curtain, smiling politely at the young woman perched on the end of the bed. 'It's Tanya Harvey, is it?'

'That's right.' The young woman tossed back her streaked blond hair and regarded Heather sourly. 'I thought they said in the papers that the health service had improved recently. Do you know how long I've been waiting to be seen? Over two hours, and it's just not good enough!'

'Unfortunately, we are extremely busy in this department.' Heather gave the young woman no opportunity to complain further as she picked up the clipboard and quickly read her admission notes. 'I see that you have a sore throat, Miss Harvey. Don't you think it would have been more sensible to visit your GP's surgery rather than the accident and emergency unit?'

'It's closed on Saturday afternoons which is why I came here.' Tanya glared at her. 'I hope you're not refusing to treat me because I know my rights....'

'I am merely pointing out that this department is for the treatment of urgent cases. It isn't an alternative to visiting your general practitioner's surgery outside of normal working hours.'

Heather took her penlight out of her top pocket and switched it on before the girl could reply. 'If you'd just open your mouth so I can take a look at your throat.'

She quickly examined the woman and wasn't surprised to discover that although Tanya Harvey's throat was red and a little swollen, there was nothing to indicate the problem was serious. Mild antibiotics would clear up the infection so she washed her hands then wrote out a prescription and handed it to her.

'These should clear up the problem but make sure you finish the full course of tablets,' she explained coolly. 'One tablet to be taken three times a day with water.'

'And where am I supposed to get them from?' Tanya demanded belligerently. 'It's gone six now and the chemist's shop will be shut. Can't you just give me the tablets?'

'I'm afraid we don't dispense antibiotics from this department. The hospital has its own dispensary in the foyer which is open until nine p.m. Take the prescription there and they will sort it out for you.'

Heather could tell that the young woman was about to say something else—another complaint, no doubt. However, just then Rob Bryce, their newly acquired houseman, poked his head round the curtain.

'Sorry to interrupt, Heather, but we've got an emergency on the way in. ETA five minutes.'

'That's OK, Rob. I'd just finished here.' With a last, brief nod at the young woman, Heather followed Rob out to the corridor. 'What do we know so far?'

'A three-year-old child trapped in a house fire.' Rob scanned the scrap of paper in his hand, mercifully missing her swiftly indrawn breath. 'Doesn't appear to be too badly burnt from what the paramedics say but he's suffering from smoke inhalation, as is the fireman who rescued him, apparently. They're bringing him in as well.'

'I see.' Heather managed to control her expression but burns cases were the most difficult of all for her to deal with. She ran her hand over her honey-brown hair to smooth a few stray wisps back into the neat chignon she favoured for work then let her hand fall to her side when she realised it was trembling. Stewart had been involved in a fire, too....

She blanked out the thought.

'Get onto the burns unit and put them on standby in case we need their input. Sometimes the severity of a burn isn't immediately apparent. And you'll need to phone the canteen and ask Ben and Melanie to come back down. We're going to need everyone available if we have two patients to deal with. We're running on minimum staffing as it is.'

She ran a quick mental check-list of what needed doing, knowing from experience that it would be easier to deal with the situation if she focused on practicalities. 'Ask Abby to check Resus and make sure that we have enough dressings and saline. Stocks were running low last time I was in there. Also get her to contact Ambulance Control and check if there are any more casualties expected. On second thoughts, I'll do that myself.'

'Will do.' Rob hurried away, muttering under his breath as he tried to remember everything he'd been asked to do. It was only his third day in the job and Heather knew how over-whelming it was to be thrown in at the deep end this way.

Normally, they only accepted housemen who had gained experience in one of the other departments, but there had been a shortage of suitable candidates so they'd had no option but to take Rob fresh from med school. He seemed to be shaping up well enough but Heather made a note to keep an eye on him. An emergency like this could be extremely harrowing for everyone involved.

Once again, she steered her mind away from what might confront her in a few minutes' time. She quickly dialled through to Ambulance Control and breathed a sigh of relief when they assured her that there were no more casualties on their way. It would be just the child and the fireman to deal with.

The sound of a siren alerted her to the fact that the ambulance was drawing up outside. Heather replaced the receiver and took a deep breath. She had to put aside her personal demons. There were people depending on her and she mustn't let them down.

'OK, Ross, I'm going to take you straight through to Resus. They'll soon get you sorted out.'

Ross eased the oxygen mask away from his face. His throat felt raw and swollen as a result of all the smoke he'd swallowed but he was less concerned about himself than the child. 'Don't worry about me. Just make sure the kid is attended to.'

'I think you can safely leave it up to us to prioritise treatment. Now, if you would put that mask back on…'

A cool hand brushed his cheek as the oxygen mask was firmly fitted back into place. Startled, Ross glanced round but the woman had already moved away. He just had time to catch a glimpse of a slender back beneath the folds of a crisp white coat before she disappeared through swing doors at the far side of the room, but it was enough to intrigue him. Who was she?

He might have attempted to voice the question out loud but the woman's intervention seemed to have galvanised the paramedics into action. Before Ross knew what was happening he found himself being wheeled through the same doors into what was obviously the resuscitation unit.

His gaze skimmed around the room and he felt a ripple run through him when he spotted a familiar white-coated figure bending over one of the beds. Once again the woman had her back to him and Ross found himself willing her to turn round as the paramedics got him safely ensconced on another bed. He had no idea why he should be so fascinated by her but he was desperate to know who she was.

His view was suddenly interrupted when a nurse appeared and began attaching him to the state-of-the-art monitoring equipment standing beside the bed. Adhesive pads were stuck to his chest and an array of electrodes clipped into place, then his finger was clamped with a plastic peg and the monitor was switched on. The young nurse smiled reassuringly as she adjusted the settings on the machine.

'Dr Carlisle will be here in a moment to check you over. Don't worry. You're going to be fine.'

Ross tried to smile back but it was difficult to perform any facial manoeuvres with the mask biting into his nose and mouth. It was starting to make him feel a bit claustrophobic but he wasn't sure it would be wise to remove it again and maybe earn himself another rebuke....

His pulse leapt as the woman across the room suddenly turned and he got his first proper look at her face. He blinked because his eyes were still a little hazy from all the smoke...or, at least, he *assumed* that was what was wrong with them. Surely it was the only explanation for why it felt as though he was looking at the face of an angel rather than a real, live, flesh-and-blood woman?

In a dazzled sweep Ross drank in each of her features from the generous curve of her mouth to the wonderfully soft grey eyes in their frame of sooty black lashes. Her nose was short and straight, her forehead smooth and unlined, her cheekbones so perfect that surely only a sculptor could have created them.

Her golden-brown hair was twisted into an uncompromising knot at the back of her head, but the severe style simply high-lighted her beauty rather than detracted from it. It also made his palms tingle in the strangest way to imagine how it would feel to pull out all those pins and allow her hair to tumble around her shoulders in wanton disarray....

She turned away when one of the nurses came back with a bag of saline. Ross sucked in as deep a breath as his swollen throat and burning lungs would allow. What the hell was going on? Why had this unknown woman had such an effect on him? Was it all the smoke he'd inhaled that had addled his brain?

He closed his eyes and forced himself to concentrate on the mundane matter of keeping a steady supply of oxygen flowing into his body. But it was alarming how that beautiful face seemed to have impinged on his consciousness. Even with his eyes closed he could still see her...his very own, very beautiful angel.

'Not as bad as I'd feared. I'd like the burns reg to take a look at this area above his left ankle but, apart from that, he's been extremely lucky.'

Heather was pleased to hear how calm she sounded. In truth, she didn't feel at all calm yet the panic that was welling inside her didn't owe itself purely to the stress of dealing with this type of emergency. What was it about the way that fireman had been looking at her that had *unsettled* her so?

She summoned a smile for the little boy lying on the bed, hoping that the rest of the team hadn't noticed anything amiss. Ben Carlisle was attending to the fireman so at least she wouldn't have to deal with him, which was a relief. Deliberately, she blocked him from her mind.

'You've been a really brave boy, Damien. Nurse is going to give you some special medicine to stop your leg hurting and then another doctor will come and see you.'

'Want my mummy,' the little boy wailed, his eyes filling with tears.

'I know you do, poppet.' Heather gently patted his hand then glanced at Melanie. 'Is his mother waiting outside? It might be better if we let her come and sit with him. There's no point in him getting upset.'

'She didn't come with him.' Melanie lowered her voice so the child couldn't overhear. 'From what I could gather she'd gone out and left him in the flat on his own. A neighbour alerted the fire crew when they arrived and told them the child was still inside the building.'

'But he's only a baby!' Heather found it impossible to hide her dismay. 'How on earth could any mother leave a child that age on his own?'

'No idea, but it happens all too often, I'm afraid.' Melanie glanced across the room and sighed. 'Evidently, the fireman who rescued him was lucky not to be killed. The whole place caved in just seconds after he got the kid out.'

Heather shuddered, unable to stop the rapid play of images that flashed through her head. They were part of the nightmare that had haunted her since Stewart had died. Everyone had said that he'd been a hero but it was hard to find comfort in that fact when all she could think about was what she had lost that day.

'Heather, are you OK?'

'Fine. I was just wondering if we should ask the police to find the mother,' she said briskly when she heard the concern in Melanie's voice. She mustn't think about what had happened to Stewart. She must focus on what needed doing, instead of allowing her emotions to run away with her. 'If they questioned the neighbours then someone might be able to tell them where she went.'

'Want me to have word with them?' Melanie offered. 'There's a policeman waiting outside so I could ask him.'

'No. It's OK. I'll do it. The burns reg should be here any minute....' Heather glanced round as the door opened and Alan Fontain appeared. 'Ah, here he is now.'

She quickly relayed everything that had been done for the little boy for the benefit of the other registrar. Alan was of the same opinion as her, that the child had been extremely fortunate to have got off with such a small area of damage. He made arrangements to admit Damien to the burns unit then hurriedly left.

'If you'll take Damien to the burns unit, Mel, I'll have a word with that policeman,' Heather began, only to stop once more when Ben approached her.

'Would you mind taking a look at this chap for me, Heather? I don't think the damage is too severe but I've not handled any cases like this before and I'd hate to miss anything.'

The young registrar's handsome face broke into a rueful smile. Ben had caused quite a stir since he'd started working in the accident and emergency unit but, so far as Heather was aware, he'd not asked any of the nurses out yet. 'The effect of smoke inhalation is not something you see very often in the maternity unit, which was my last rotation!'

'I don't suppose it is,' Heather conceded, trying to hide her dismay. However, the fact that she should feel the least bit worried about dealing with a patient alarmed her. What *was* it about this patient that disturbed her so much?

'I'll ask the police to chase up the mother,' Melanie put in helpfully, shooting a megawatt smile at Ben.

'Thanks.' Heather formed her mouth into a smile but her lips felt as though they'd been turned to rubber all of a sudden. She would have to help Ben, of course, because it would be unforgivable to endanger a patient's life by missing some vital sign which the younger doctor had overlooked.

In silence she crossed the room and took the notes Ben handed her, using the few moments it took to read through them to calm her racing heart. Then, when she could delay no longer, she handed back the clipboard and turned to the man lying on the bed.

'My name is Heather Cooper and I'm the senior registrar in the accident and emergency unit.'

She couldn't have counted the number of times she had introduced herself that very same way, yet for some reason the words sounded unfamiliar, as though it was the first time she'd ever said them, the first time they had really *mattered*.

Her shocked grey eyes flew to the man's face and stopped, held by the expression in the hazel ones which were regarding her with exactly the same degree of bewilderment. In that moment Heather knew that it wasn't her imagination that something odd was going on because he could feel it, too. And the panic she'd felt before was nothing to the fear that suddenly gripped her.

There was no room in her life for another hero!

CHAPTER TWO

'IF YOU could just lean forward, Mr Tanner…a little more. That's fine. Thank you.'

Ross felt his rigid muscles relax as the cool fingers that had been touching his bare back were suddenly removed. Dr Heather Cooper's examination had been extremely thorough, although he wasn't foolish enough to imagine that he should read anything into it. Even though he knew nothing about her, he sensed that she would treat all her patients the same way. Dr Cooper was just very good at her job.

Disbelief shot through him and the monitor blipped as his heart rate increased. He saw Heather Cooper's eyes swivel towards the screen and willed himself to calm down. The last thing he wanted was for her to suspect that something was wrong with him, but it was hard to deal with the way he seemed to be behaving all of a sudden.

Since when had he developed the gift of ESP? How on earth could he *know* that Heather was good at her job? He had no idea but it was worrying enough to cause his heart to fit in several more beats in rapid succession.

'Do you have any chest pain at all?'

Dr Cooper's calm voice should have been the perfect antidote to his fanciful musings but Ross was past the point of no return by that stage. Blip, blip, blip went the damned machine as he shook his head, seemingly intent on making a liar of him.

'Are you quite sure, Mr Tanner?'

Those cool fingers returned to hold the chilly end of a stethoscope against his chest. Ross sucked in as much oxygen as his burning lungs would allow but the blasted machine rattled out another volley of blips. Heaven help him if Heather Cooper worked out that the reason why his heart was hopping up and

16

down like a kid on a pogo stick was because *she* was touching him!

'Relax, Mr Tanner. I know how worrying this must be for you but I'm confident that you've suffered only minimal damage to your throat and lungs....'

She stopped talking while she listened, lightly holding the end of the stethoscope against his chest with the tips of her fingers. Ross focused on the pale ovals of her nails because that seemed a relatively harmless thing to do. Fingernails weren't the least bit scary. Neither were they sexy, although Heather Cooper's nails were *particularly* beautiful with those delicate half-moons at the base of each shimmering through the unvarnished shell-pink.

Ross saw her stiffen as his heart gave an almighty surge. He closed his eyes, praying that nobody would notice the matching response that had occurred in another part of his body. Thankfully, the nurse had only removed his shirt and he was still wearing his uniform trousers beneath the sheet. With a bit of luck they would save him from any major embarrassment.

'We'll monitor what's happening overnight.'

Ross's eyes flew open when he realised that Heather Cooper was speaking to him. She was calmly rolling up her stethoscope but there was a hint of colour in her cheeks that hadn't been apparent before. His gaze dipped down then swooped back up in relief when he realised that the bulky trousers had safely preserved his modesty. If Dr Cooper was looking a little hot under the collar then it had nothing to do with him.

'I'm glad I asked you for a second opinion, Heather.'

Ross's eyes swivelled to the young man standing beside Heather Cooper and he felt a sudden stab of irritation. The fellow was gazing at her like a lovesick puppy! Didn't he understand that a mature and intelligent woman like Heather wouldn't be swayed by a good-looking face, that she needed a man of her own age and experience to satisfy her needs? A woman of Heather's calibre wouldn't look twice at someone several years her junior.

Would she?

Ross's stomach sank when it struck him that he was making an awful lot of assumptions he wasn't qualified to make. How could *he* say what Heather Cooper needed? Maybe that blush on her face was a direct result of working side by side with the handsome younger doctor? Maybe the pair were already involved in a relationship and being able to work together added an extra buzz?

He'd watched enough hospital dramas on television while he'd been working night shifts to know there must be *some* basis for portraying hospitals as hotbeds of romance. Maybe the beautiful Dr Cooper and the handsome Dr Carlisle were starring in their very own series. *Love in the Accident and Emergency Unit.*

Hell's teeth!

'It's always safer to get a second opinion in a case like this, Ben.'

Heather smiled at the young registrar, praying that he couldn't tell how on edge she felt. Was it her imagination or had the tension level suddenly upped several degrees?

She glanced at Abby McLeod, the sister in charge of the A and E unit that shift, and was relieved to receive a calm smile in return. Abby obviously hadn't noticed anything amiss so it must be her imagination. Time to knock this on the head. Once Ross Tanner was off their hands then she could get back to normal.

Hopefully…

Heather blanked out that last thought by dint of sheer will-power. She turned to Ross Tanner again, finding it less stressful to focus strictly on professional matters. Tanner was a patient and it was her job to treat him as such.

'I can find no indication of there being anything wrong with your heart, Mr Tanner, but, as I said, I shall recommend that you be kept on a monitor overnight.' She shrugged. 'We would have kept you in until we were sure that your lungs were clear so it's simply a matter of attaching you to a bit more machinery.'

'I had a medical last week and my heart and everything else that matters were fine.'

Ross Tanner had eased the mask away from his mouth. Heather just managed to suppress a shiver when she heard his voice for the first time. Although the swelling in his throat would have caused some changes to its tone, she guessed that he normally had a wonderfully deep voice. She was overcome by a sudden desire to hear how it sounded once he'd recovered before she briskly dismissed the idea. Once Ross Tanner left Resus that would be the last she saw of him.

'That's good to hear, Mr Tanner.' It was hard to ignore how disquieting she found that idea but Heather had become an expert at controlling her feelings. 'I know how rigorous the fire brigade's medical examinations are and can only repeat that I don't believe there is a problem with your heart. It's purely a precaution, you understand.'

'The old belt and braces approach?' Ross Tanner grinned at her, his teeth gleaming whitely through his smoke-blackened skin, his hazel eyes sparkling with amusement. 'Well, I certainly can't argue with that approach, Dr Cooper. If there's one thing the brigade teaches you, it's always to try and minimise any risks.'

'I would have thought that was impossible in your job,' she said tartly, praying that he couldn't tell how mixed up she was feeling. Why on earth had her heart started racing because Tanner had smiled at her? What could it mean?

'Surely every time you attend a fire you're putting yourself at risk? The unexpected can always happen and nobody—*nobody*—can guarantee that it won't!'

Heather only realised that she'd raised her voice when she saw the startled expressions on everyone's faces. She took a deep breath but it was hard to pretend nothing was wrong and pointless, too, when everyone could tell just by looking at her that she was upset.

'I'm sorry. I didn't mean to upset you.'

Ross Tanner reached over and touched her hand, just lightly, but it was still too much. Her emotions were too raw at that moment to withstand anyone's sympathy and especially not his. Heather jerked her hand away and turned from the bed, ignoring Ben's look of concern as she brushed past him.

'Phone the bed manager and tell him that we have a patient who needs admitting, please. I'm taking my break now but page me if anything urgent crops up.'

She didn't wait to hear what Ben said in reply. She strode to the door but was forced to stop when Melanie and a porter came back with the trolley they'd used to take Damien to the burns unit. Heather waited while they wheeled it into the room then hurried out of the door, cursing under her breath when the hem of her white coat snagged on a rough splinter of wood.

She stopped to disentangle herself, automatically glancing round and shaking her head when Melanie offered to help. Through the gap in the doors she could see Ross Tanner watching her and her heart felt as though it was going to burst right out of her chest when she saw the compassion in his eyes. He knew that comment she'd made about the unexpected happening had been based on experience. He had recognised her pain and empathised with it. He wanted to help her.

The idea terrified her. The last thing Heather wanted was to talk about what had happened to Stewart. She couldn't deal with the heartache it would unleash all over again. She needed to keep this pain safely locked away inside her. Opening her heart to Ross Tanner wasn't an option.

'Hey! I thought those were supposed to be for me?'

Ross upended the paper bag and sighed when a solitary grape dropped onto the bed. 'Thanks, guys—I don't think!'

'Blame Jack. He said there was no point giving you grapes because you wouldn't be able to swallow them with your throat. He said he might as well save you a job.' Terry Green grinned as he drew up a chair and sat down, but Ross could see the troubled light in the older man's eyes.

It was way past evening visiting hours but the crew from Red Watch had managed to persuade the ward sister to let them in to see him. Fortunately, Ross had been put in a side room off the main ward and the only other occupant—an elderly man—was watching television in the lounge. At least he didn't need to feel guilty about disturbing anyone. He seemed to have caused enough upset for one day.

He forced himself to concentrate on what Terry was saying, but the pain he'd glimpsed in Heather Cooper's eyes had haunted him. There was no doubt in his mind that something dreadful had happened to Heather in the past and he resolved to find out all he could about it, although why he should be so interested was beyond him. However, if there was one thing Ross had learned to do it was to trust his instincts, and his instincts were telling him that this mattered. A lot.

'I had no idea you'd turned back. One minute you were right behind me and the next time I looked you'd disappeared.' Terry shook his head in dismay. He was obviously having a hard time dealing with what had gone on earlier that day.

'I said that you needed your hearing testing,' Jack Marsh—another of the crew—chipped in. 'You have the telly turned up that loud in the break room that you have to be going deaf, and this just proves it!'

'It was my fault,' Ross cut in before a squabble could break out. Tensions always ran high after a member of the team was injured and he didn't want to be the cause of an argument. 'I was following you out, Terry, when I glimpsed something out of the corner of my eye and went to check it out. I should have told you what I was doing but there wasn't time.'

'Damn good job you did—check it out, I mean.' Jack popped the last grape into his mouth and chewed it. 'Another minute and the kid would have had it. The cupboard where you found him, Ross, ended up in the basement.'

There was a moment's silence as they all reflected on how close the child had come to being killed that day. Most of the men at Hexton fire station had children of their own and it was easy for them to imagine how they would have felt.

At thirty-six, Ross still hadn't found the right woman to settle down with and start a family, although he certainly hadn't ruled out the chance of it happening. He loved kids and adored

his sister's twin boys. However, he was realistic enough to
know that a woman who committed herself to a man who did
the kind of job he did would have to be very special. Living
with the risks involved was something he had long since accepted, but he'd seen too many relationships break up during
his time with the brigade not to realise the toll it took. Would
Heather Cooper be able to handle it?

He coughed as the question caught him unawares. Although
his throat was feeling a little easier, his lungs were still very
sensitive. He accepted the oxygen mask Terry handed him,
relieved that his expression was concealed by the opaque plastic.

What would the guys say if they discovered he was having
thoughts like that about a woman he'd met just a few hours
ago? They'd probably think the smoke had affected his reasoning and maybe they'd be right, too. Heather Cooper wasn't
interested in him, as she had made abundantly clear.

That thought was a little too close to the truth not to cause
him some discomfort. As Ross drew in a few more breaths of
oxygen his mind raced back over what had happened in the
Resus room. Did Heather really have something going with that
junior doctor?

He tried to recall their body language even though he could
scarcely believe he was doing anything so *pathetic*. He had a
book full of phone numbers back at his flat, most of them
belonging to women who were every bit as beautiful and de-
sirable as Heather Cooper was. And yet when was the last time
that he'd called any of them?

It was alarming to realise that it must be a good six months
since he'd been out on a date and that he couldn't for the life
of him remember who with, let alone where they had gone.
Yet here he was, lying in a hospital bed and trying to remember
exactly how Heather Cooper had looked at another man.

Ross swallowed his groan of dismay but now that he'd set
off down this route it was impossible to stop. Heather's beautiful face swam before his eyes, that cool little smile curling
her generous mouth. It hadn't appeared to warm up by even

half a degree when she'd looked at her junior colleague, but maybe she preferred to be discreet about their relationship?

The fire brigade certainly frowned on liaisons between the sexes and took immediate steps to transfer the people involved to different stations. Maybe Heather was afraid that young Dr Carlisle might be given his marching orders if their affair became public knowledge so preferred to keep things low-key?

Ross sighed as he realised that he might very well be right, although Heather hadn't given the impression of a woman enjoying a heady love affair when she'd left Resus. His heart ached as he recalled the suffering on her face. It made him wonder once again what kind of a tragedy had befallen her in the past and what he could do to help her get over it.

He sucked in another lungful of air but the facts had to be faced. Why should he imagine that Heather Cooper needed *his* help?

'And the little puppy snuggled up in his basket and fell fast asleep.'

Heather closed the book and quietly placed it on the bedside cabinet. Standing up, she tucked the quilt around her small daughter, feeling a wave of love wash over her as she looked at the sleeping child.

Grace had just turned two and each day she grew more like Stewart to look at. She had Stewart's mop of dark brown curls, the same deep blue eyes and wonderful smile. Grace was living proof of their love for one another, the child they had both longed for. How proud Stewart would have been of his tiny daughter.

Tears stung Heather's eyes and she quickly blinked them away as she bent to turn off the lamp. She hadn't allowed herself to cry since Grace had been born and she had no intention of breaking her rule now. She didn't want Grace to grow up surrounded by sadness. Far better to keep her emotions in check rather than let them affect her precious daughter, even though today it was proving unusually difficult. Had it anything to do with meeting Ross Tanner, perhaps?

'Supper's ready, Heather.'

Heather jumped as her mother, Sandra, popped her head round the bedroom door. She tried to dismiss the idea as she followed the older woman to the kitchen but the thought that Ross Tanner might have had an effect on how she had behaved alarmed her. She didn't even *know* the man so how could he be responsible for her loss of self-control?

'It's only shepherd's pie, I'm afraid. I didn't get a chance to go to the supermarket.'

'It's fine, Mum.' Heather sat at the table and took the plate Sandra handed her with a grateful smile. 'I'm only glad that I don't have to set to and start making a meal for myself when I get home from work. You spoil me, you know that, don't you?'

'If I can't spoil my own daughter then who can I spoil?' Sandra said lightly, taking her own seat.

'Your granddaughter?' Heather laughed when her mother grimaced. 'Grace told me that you'd taken her to see the ducks after nursery school. And then she did just happen to mention something about going on the swings as well.'

'I enjoy playing with her. Anyway, the playground is on our way home and you meet a lot of nice people there, too.'

Heather frowned when she saw a little colour run up her mother's cheeks. If she wasn't mistaken, Sandra was blushing. She put down her knife and fork and stared at her.

'These nice people you meet—is there anyone in particular you're referring to?'

'Well, yes, actually.' Sandra stared at her plate for a moment then seemed to make up her mind. 'There's this very nice man who I've met at the playground a number of times. He's a widower and he has a little grandson. He…well, he asked me if I'd like to go out for a drink with him one night.'

'Did he indeed? And what did you say?' Heather hid her surprise because it was the first time that her mother had shown any interest in socialising since she'd moved to London to help her look after Grace.

Heather's parents had divorced when she'd been in her teens

and her father had remarried shortly afterwards and moved to California with his new wife. Apart from a yearly Christmas card, Heather had very little contact with him.

Her mother had never remarried although she'd had a wide circle of friends of both sexes back home in Manchester. It suddenly struck Heather how much Sandra had given up when she'd moved to London, and how lonely she must have been without her friends. How selfish of her not to have thought about that before.

'I hope you said yes, Mum.' She reached over the table and squeezed Sandra's hand. 'It's about time you went out and had some fun!'

'So you think it's all right for me to accept, then?' Sandra sounded worried. 'I told David—that's his name, David Harper—that I would need to think about it first, you see.'

'What on earth is there to think about?' Heather regarded her mother sternly. 'Tell him that you'll go, Mum. That's an order!'

'All right, I will.' Sandra squared her shoulders then looked steadily at Heather. 'But what you just said, about it being time I had some fun, applies to you, too, darling. Stewart wouldn't want you to grieve for ever. He'd want you to get on with your life and make the most of it.'

'That's exactly what I'm doing.' Heather picked up her fork. She swallowed a mouthful of mashed potato but it tasted like sawdust all of a sudden.

'There's more to life than working and looking after Grace,' Sandra said quietly, then changed the subject to what Grace had done after they had arrived home that afternoon.

Heather made appropriate responses but she couldn't seem to give her small daughter's antics her undivided attention as she usually did. Was her mother right? Was it time that she looked for more out of life than just her work and caring for Grace?

Her mind veered off towards what that *more* might entail and she felt her heart spasm in panic. She wouldn't risk falling in love again! Even if she found a man who could match

Stewart in her estimation—which was highly unlikely—she couldn't do it. She couldn't face the heartache if anything happened to him, too. What she'd said to that fireman today about the unexpected happening had been true. He, more than anyone, must know that.

In Ross Tanner's world life and death were too closely linked to be discounted. It made her wonder how any woman could bear to fall in love with a man who put himself in constant danger like that. How did a woman cope with the thought that the man she loved might not come home one day? She certainly couldn't, which made it all the more imperative that she steer clear of Tanner.

The thought brought her up short. She wouldn't see Ross Tanner again so what was she worrying about? They had fleetingly crossed paths that day and that was the end of the matter.

Heather shivered as the cool finger of premonition suddenly slid down her spine. Or had it been merely the beginning and not the end?

'Thanks, Jane. I really appreciate everything you've done for me.'

Ross kissed the ward sister's cheek. It was Monday morning and, after a lot of persuasion on his behalf, he'd finally been discharged. The consultant had been inclined to keep him in another day but in the end he'd relented after Ross had promised to come straight back if he experienced any problems. To his mind, it was a lot of fuss about nothing, but he did appreciate the excellent care he'd received.

He left the ward and headed for the lift. He knew that he could have asked any one of the crew from Red Watch to collect him but he'd decided to take a taxi back to his flat. Maybe he was making a big mistake but there was something he needed to do before he left.

Sign boards directed him to the accident and emergency unit when he reached the ground floor so he had no difficulty finding his way. The waiting area was packed with people and Ross hesitated. Maybe this wasn't a good time to talk to Heather when she was so busy.

The thought had barely crossed his mind when he spotted her leaving a cubicle and, without pausing to reconsider, he hurried after her. 'Heather!'

It seemed the most natural thing in the world to call out her first name, natural and right. Dr Cooper was too formal, Ms Cooper impolite, so how else would he address her? And yet Ross wasn't prepared for the way it made him feel as her name rolled off his tongue. *Heather.*

He repeated it in his head and felt the heat that flowed through him as he savoured it once more. In that moment Ross knew that it might have been the first time he'd said it but it wouldn't be the last. Definitely not!

He saw her turn, saw the alarm that lit her soft grey eyes when she recognised him, and knew that it wasn't going to be easy to convince *her* of that. Given an inch, Heather was going to run a mile in the opposite direction both physically and metaphorically speaking. He had to find a way to stop her, had to make her run towards him instead of away. Only then could either of them be truly happy.

'I'm busy.'

The clipped tone of her voice cut through his thoughts like a hot knife slicing through butter, and he flinched. He wasn't a man given to fanciful notions normally and it stunned him to find himself indulging in them now. However, he didn't have the time to worry about it when he had more important matters to deal with, like making Heather listen to him for starters. From the look on her face, listening to anything he had to say was about as attractive an idea as plunging her hand into a nest of vipers!

'I realise that so I won't detain you. I just wanted to thank you for what you did the other day, Heather. For me and the kid. I believe he's on the mend.'

'Yes, so I believe.'

Her expression softened so that Ross had a glimpse of the real woman beneath the ice-cool exterior. He sent up a silent vote of thanks that he was no longer attached to any monitors when he felt his heart kick up a storm. Did she have any idea how drop-dead gorgeous she was? he wondered giddily.

He cleared his throat but he could hear how rough his voice sounded even if Heather seemed blissfully unaware of the strain he was under. Keeping his hands by his sides and well away from her took an awful lot of will-power.

'You did a great job on him, and on me, too. I just wanted to find a way to thank you properly and wondered if you'd consider having dinner with me one night.'

Ross was almost as shocked as Heather so obviously was when the invitation sprang from his lips. He certainly hadn't planned on asking her out and would have set about it with a bit more finesse if he had. He saw her face close up and cursed his wayward tongue because it had just cost him an awful lot of ground he might never be able to make up.

'Thank you, but that isn't necessary, Mr Tanner. I was only doing my job. Now, if you'll excuse me.'

She didn't wait for him to reply before she hurried away. Ross didn't try to stop her because there was no point. He had wasted the one and only opportunity he was likely to get and that was it. *Finito.*

There was a taxi dropping off a fare outside the main entrance. Ross got in and told the driver to take him home. He sank back in the seat as the cab headed down the drive, feeling so bad that he seriously wondered if he should have stayed in hospital after all. There was an ache in his chest which alarmed him until he realised it was disappointment at ruining his chance to get to know Heather and not the prelude to a heart attack. He wouldn't get another opportunity…unless he came up with some sort of a plan to engineer another meeting with her.

A brilliant smile suddenly lit his face and a middle-aged woman, who had stopped on the kerb to let the taxi pass, blushed with pleasure as she received the full benefit of it. Ross didn't notice her smiling back at him because he was too concerned about devising the perfect plan to see Heather again. It wouldn't be easy but he'd find a way. There was too much at stake to fail!

CHAPTER THREE

'WE'LL need to X-ray your wrist, Mrs Montgomery. I'm fairly certain that it's broken and not just badly sprained, as you hoped.'

Heather smiled reassuringly at the elderly woman. Alice Montgomery had tripped over a paving stone whilst out shopping with her husband. The couple were obviously shocked by the accident so she decided to arrange for a porter to take the old lady to the radiography unit rather than ask her husband to take her. There was a small unit attached to the accident and emergency department so Alice shouldn't have to wait too long to be seen.

'I'll get a porter to take you through to X-Ray. You can go with your wife, Mr Montgomery, or you can wait in Reception. I could ask one of the nurses to fetch you a cup of tea,' she suggested, noticing how grey the old man looked.

'It's very kind of you, Doctor, but I'd prefer to go with Alice. We do everything together, you see.'

'Of course. Why don't you sit there and keep your wife company until the porter gets here? It could take a few minutes to find one who's free.'

Heather left the cubicle but instead of going directly to the phone to summon a porter she went to the staffroom instead. Melanie was in there, making herself a cup of tea, and Heather smiled beseechingly at her.

'Any chance that you'd make a cup of tea for the old man in cubicle six? He's really shaken up and it might help to steady him. I'd make it myself only I'm a bit pushed this morning with Ben being off sick.'

'No problem,' Melanie replied cheerfully, dropping a tea-bag into a second mug and topping it up with boiling water from the kettle. 'What's up with Ben, by the way? Any idea?'

'He's suffering from a nasty case of diarrhoea apparently. Trish took the message.' Heather grimaced. 'Let's hope it isn't catching. The last thing we need is the rest of the staff going down with some bug or other.'

'I doubt that will happen. Ben doesn't get close enough to pass on his germs,' Melanie observed ruefully.

Heather laughed. 'I take it that you've had no luck with him?'

'Nope! Not even a flicker of interest. I don't know what I'm doing wrong. Maybe you could give me a few tips?'

'Tips?' Heather stared at the younger woman in surprise. 'What do you mean?'

'That if I had the same kind of effect on our dishy Dr Carlisle that you had on that fireman, I'd be a happy woman.'

Melanie picked up the mug of tea and headed for the door. She grinned as she eased past Heather. 'I saw him talking to you, Heather. He'd obviously made a special detour down here to see you.'

'I...um... Yes.'

Heather blushed. She'd tried to forget about Ross Tanner's visit by concentrating on work, but Melanie's teasing comment brought it all flooding back. She had been so shocked when he'd asked her out to dinner that she'd not even stopped to think. Her refusal had been instinctive yet all of a sudden she found herself wondering *why* Ross had invited her out. Had it been simply his way of thanking her, as he'd claimed, or because he was attracted to her, as Melanie believed?

The thought made Heather blush all the more and she heard Melanie laugh. 'There's nothing like a hero to make a woman go weak at the knees, is there, Heather?'

Fortunately Melanie didn't wait for her to reply as she hurried away with the tea. Heather followed more slowly, taking several calming breaths to get herself under control. Maybe some women were attracted to the heroic type of man but she wasn't one of them. If...and it was a very big *if*...she ever formed another relationship with a man then she would make sure he was someone who spent his working life safely en-sconced behind a desk.

She had reached for the phone to ring for a porter when it struck her that a few days ago she wouldn't even have consid-ered another relationship. She'd had her work and Grace and they had been more than enough. Her throat constricted with a sudden attack of nerves. Although she hated to admit it, she couldn't deny that meeting Ross Tanner seemed to have af-fected her thinking. What a good job it was that she'd refused his invitation to dinner.

It was Friday before Ross came up with a plan to see Heather again. It had been a busy week and Red Watch had been called out a number of times while they'd been on duty. They were off duty that weekend and Ross was looking forward to spend-ing some time with his sister, Kate, and his nephews. It made a nice change, being part of a family, even if it was only for a couple of days.

The plan occurred to him while he was catching up with some of the never-ending paperwork. A memo from divisional HQ, reminding station officers about the need to keep on top of issuing fire certificates, had the same effect as a light being switched on. When was St Gertrude's due for an inspection?

A quick check of the files told him that the hospital was scheduled for a visit that very month. Ross closed the filing cabinet drawer with a satisfied smile. If he could time his visit to coincide with when Heather was on duty, that would be the perfect opportunity to speak to her again. She couldn't refuse to co-operate because all public buildings required an up-to-date fire certificate. And whilst he was dealing with the essen-tials he would try to draw her out. If he could just get past her defences then he might be able to get to know her better.

He sighed because there was no reason to imagine that Heather would want to get to know him.

*   *   *

Saturday was cool and blustery, a brisk May breeze sending the clouds scudding across the sky. Heather was off for the whole weekend but she was up before seven and had time to shower and dress in jeans and a long-sleeved navy T-shirt before Grace woke.

She took the little girl into the kitchen and popped her in her high chair then gave her some cereal. It was always a treat to be able to have breakfast with her daughter because most days she was in such a rush to get to work that she had to leave it to her mother to feed and dress Grace. It worried Heather that she was unable to spend very much time with the little girl but Grace seemed happy and well adjusted and there was little else she could do when she needed to earn a living.

Sandra came in just as Heather was wiping Grace's hands. She dropped a kiss on her granddaughter's curls then smiled at Heather. 'You two are early birds this morning. You make me feel quite guilty.'

'Rubbish! It's about time you had a lie-in, Mum,' Heather declared, lifting Grace out of her chair. She glanced at the kitchen clock and grinned. 'Although not many folk would consider getting up at half past seven as having had a lie-in, especially at a weekend!'

Sandra laughed as she poured herself a cup of tea from the pot. 'I suppose not. Anyway, what have you got planned for today? I managed to do the grocery shopping yesterday so you don't have to worry about that.'

'Catch up with some washing then take Grace to the park if the weather stays fine.' She glanced at the little girl and smiled. 'Do you want to go and play on the swings, darling?'

'Yes!' Grace clapped her hands in delight.

Heather laughed. 'That's my day sorted out. How about you? What are you planning on doing, Mum?'

'Oh, I thought I might pop into town if you don't need me.' Sandra shrugged, feigning nonchalance. 'I'm going out with David tonight and thought I'd treat myself to something new to wear. Silly really because I've got heaps of clothes.'

'Of course it isn't silly!' Heather replied firmly. 'You want to look your best, don't you?'

'Well, yes… But it's just a drink, Heather. Nothing more than that,' Sandra said quickly.

'A drink or a meal, what's the difference? You deserve a night out, and if this David is anywhere near as nice as I imagine he is then you'll have a great time. Now, I'd better get this little madam dressed.'

With a last encouraging smile at Sandra, Heather left the room. She was really glad that her mother had decided to accept David Harper's invitation. It was about time Sandra went out and enjoyed herself instead of staying at home all the time. Just for a second the memory of Ross Tanner's invitation came flooding back before she quickly dismissed it. She had turned him down and she'd been right to do so. She didn't need that kind of a complication in her life.

Ross arrived at his sister's house at eleven and by ten minutes past the hour he was on his way to the park with his nephews. According to his sister, the twins had been watching for his car since they'd finished their breakfast and he didn't have the heart to make them wait any longer.

His sister was seven months pregnant and suffering from high blood pressure. She'd been ordered to rest by her GP, no easy feat with two lively five-year-olds to look after. Mike, his brother-in-law, was working in the Arab Emirates for one of the oil companies. Although he was due to fly home for the birth of the new baby, his absence hadn't helped the situation.

Ross did what he could and Kate's friends rallied round as well—doing the school run and fetching the weekly grocery shopping for her—but trips to the playground had had to be curtailed. Consequently, Josh and Luke could hardly wait to get there.

Ross helped the boys clamber onto adjacent swings and started pushing them. The playground was busy with it being the weekend and there were children running about everywhere. He gave Luke a push and turned to do the same for Josh then felt his heart sink when he saw a small child racing towards them. The toddler obviously had no idea of the danger as she ran straight in front of the swings.

Ross heard a woman shout but he didn't pause as he darted forward and lifted the child out of the way. He could feel his heart thudding as he carried the toddler to safety because it had been such a close call. Setting the little girl on the ground, he bent down to look at her, smiling reassuringly when he saw her lower lip wobble.

'You're OK, poppet,' he began, but got no further when a woman suddenly appeared and swept the child into her arms. He felt his heart thud all the harder when he realised in surprise that it was none other than Heather Cooper.

'Grace! Are you all right, darling?' she demanded frantically. 'Tell Mummy where you're hurt.'

Ross felt a wave of compassion wash over him when he saw how terrified Heather looked. He hurried to reassure her. 'The swing didn't hit her, Heather. She might be a bit scared because I grabbed hold of her but she isn't hurt.'

'Are you sure?'

Heather raised fear-darkened eyes to his and Ross could see that she was trembling. He put his hand on her shoulder and gently squeezed it, feeling the delicacy of her bones beneath the thick red fleece jacket she was wearing.

'Quite sure. She's just had a bit of a fright.'

Heather took a deep breath but Ross could hear the shrill edge of hysteria in her voice. 'It's all my fault. I should have kept tighter hold of her hand. If anything had happened to her…!'

'But it didn't.' Once again he squeezed her shoulder but her reaction alarmed him. It was natural that Heather should be upset by the thought of what could have happened to her daughter, but her response seemed to be way beyond what he would have considered as normal.

He glanced round when Luke shouted out that he and Josh wanted to go on the slide next. Maybe it had nothing to do with him but Ross knew that he couldn't just walk away and leave Heather when she was so upset. He came to a swift decision, hoping that he wouldn't ruin his chances of getting to know her better by appearing too pushy.

'Grace isn't the only one who's had a fright from the look of you. What you need is a cup of tea, Heather. I was going to take my nephews to the café for a drink, so why don't you join us?'

'Oh, no, I couldn't—' Heather began, but Ross simply wasn't prepared to leave her there on her own. She was still trembling and looked so pale that he was afraid she might pass out.

'Yes, you can.' He put his hand under her elbow and helped her to her feet, keeping firm hold of her as she settled the little girl in her arms. 'You won't do yourself or your daughter any good if you faint, will you?'

'I suppose not.'

Heather bit her lip and he could tell that she was trying to decide what to do. The fact that it was such an effort filled him with tenderness. Heather had struck him as someone who was very much in control when they'd first met and to see her having such difficulty making up her mind simply proved how shaken she was. Unconsciously, Ross's tone softened and became persuasive.

'As a doctor I imagine you must have told dozens of people the same thing over the years, that a cup of tea would do them the power of good. Now it's your turn to see if it works. I'll just get the boys off the swings then we can go and test out the theory.'

'All right,' she agreed with a tentative smile.

Ross turned away before she could see how elated it had made him feel to know that he'd managed to bring a smile to her face. He lifted Josh and Luke off the swings and explained that they would have a drink first and go on the slide later. And the whole time he was doing so it felt as though his heart was going to burst right out of his chest with delight. He had made Heather smile!

Maybe it wasn't an earth-shattering event by other people's standards but it was by his and a definite step in the right direction, too. While they were having tea, he would try to make a bit more progress towards getting to know her better.…

His spirits plummeted when it struck him that he had over-looked one major point: if Heather Cooper had a child then she probably had a husband as well. Why hadn't he considered that possibility before?

By the time they'd found an empty table in the park's crowded café, Heather was beginning to wish she hadn't agreed to Ross's suggestion. The shock of knowing that Grace could have been badly hurt if the swing had hit her had played havoc with Heather's self-control. All she really wanted was to be on her own while she calmed down but, short of causing a scene, she had no choice except to go through with this now.

'Tea, Heather?'

She jumped when Ross spoke to her, feeling her pulse race when she saw the concern on his face. She didn't want to be on the receiving end of his concern when her emotions were so near to the surface.

'Um…yes, please. Tea will be fine,' she replied as coolly as she could.

'And what will your little girl have? Juice or milk?' he continued, placing his hand lightly on Grace's head and ruffling her curls.

'Milk, please.' Heather managed to maintain her poise but it disturbed her to see how her daughter was smiling up at Ross. Grace was normally such a reserved child and rarely responded to people she didn't know. However, the little girl wasn't shy with Ross, oddly enough.

Heather frowned as she watched him turn to the two boys. Ross had told her they were his nephews and it was obvious he was very fond of them and that they adored him, too. She could tell from the easy way he behaved with the twins that he spent a lot of time with them. Maybe Grace had sensed that he was used to children and had reacted accordingly?

It was a relief to have found such a simple explanation. Heather allowed herself to relax for the first time since she'd

sat down, but maybe she'd been a bit premature about lowering
her guard. She felt her breath catch when she heard Ross laugh
at something one of the boys had said.

She looked away as Ross went to fetch their drinks, afraid
that her expression might be too revealing. Why should she
feel all warm inside just because she'd heard him laughing?
Why should she feel anything at all when Ross was, essentially,
a stranger to her?

'I think I've just about got everything.'

Ross came back with a tray full of drinks. He doled out
glasses and straws to the children then dropped a handful of
paper napkins in the centre of the table and sat down. Picking
up a packet of sugar, he tipped the contents into a cup of tea
and stirred it briskly then placed it in front of Heather with a
teasing grin.

'Hot, sweet tea. Just what the doctor ordered!'

'Thank you.' Heather picked up a spoon and stirred the tea
again even though it wasn't necessary to do so. However, the
laughter in Ross's eyes had once again played havoc with her
equilibrium. She could feel her heart thumping and it shocked
her to realise that she was so susceptible to him. She searched
for something to say to defuse the situation and her eyes
alighted on the heap of paper napkins.

'Why do you need all those napkins?'

'One thing I've learned through bitter experience is to be
prepared like any good Scout should be.'

His smiled widened and Heather felt her heart kick in another half-dozen extra beats. There was no ignoring the fact
that Ross was looking at her like a man looked at a woman he
found extremely attractive.

'The day you don't have a wad of paper napkins to hand is
the day that one of the little horrors ends up spilling orange
juice all over the place!'

'Sounds as though you spend a lot of time with your nephews,' Heather replied lightly, although it was hard to behave
as though nothing had happened.

'As much as I can, especially at the moment.' He leant back

in his chair and sighed. 'My sister is expecting another baby and she's had problems with her blood pressure. She needs to rest but it isn't easy with two lively five-year-olds to take care of and a husband who's working abroad. I do what I can whenever I have any time off.'

'She's lucky to have you to help her,' Heather said as evenly as she could. She picked up her cup and took refuge in sipping some of the hot tea. She never usually had any difficulty keeping a rein on her emotions but she'd had such a fright that day when she'd seen Grace running towards the swings. Maybe that explained why she was behaving so oddly.

'That's what families are for, isn't it?' He shrugged but she could see the curiosity in his hazel eyes as he looked at her across the table. 'I imagine it's difficult to balance the demands of your job with your daughter's needs. Does your husband help?'

Heather put the cup carefully back on its saucer because her hands had started shaking and she didn't want to spill the drink. She knew that Ross was trying to find out more about her, but how much should she tell him? Did she really want to explain about Stewart's death? Yet for some reason telling Ross the version she'd told everyone else didn't seem enough.

'I'm not married.' She cleared her throat, shocked that she should feel the need to debate the issue. What difference did it make what she told Ross? She barely knew him and she certainly wasn't under any obligation to pour out her life story to him!

'Grace's father and I were engaged but he died before she was born.'

Her tone was devoid of emotion, almost as though she was talking about someone else rather than herself. She'd learned from experience that most people didn't pry any further if she stated the facts in that indifferent way.

'How awful for you! It must have been a terrible shock.' Ross leant forward and laid his hand on top of hers. 'I can't imagine how difficult it must have been for you to cope on your own, Heather.'

The compassion in his voice was so genuine that Heather felt a lump come to her throat. 'It was awful,' she admitted huskily.

'Can you tell me what happened? It might help to talk about it. I may be wrong, of course, but I have an idea that you've been bottling up your feelings for far too long.'

He ran his thumb over the back of her hand in a gentle caress that was meant to soothe, but it had the opposite effect. Heather felt a burning heat flow through her body and start to melt away the layers of ice with which she had surrounded herself for the past few years.

She snatched her hand away, terrified by the thought of what might happen then. She didn't want to feel the way she'd felt during those terrible months after Stewart had died. She couldn't bear it! She simply couldn't cope with the heartache again. Ross might mean well but he had no idea what he was doing.

She stood up abruptly and pushed back her chair, ignoring the startled look he gave her. 'I'm sorry, but I have to go. I hadn't realised how late it is.'

Moving swiftly around the table, she lifted Grace out of the high chair, shaking her head when the little girl reached for the beaker of milk. 'I'm sorry, darling, but we have to go now. Granny is waiting for us. You can have another drink when we get home.'

Grace was obviously less than pleased about leaving her milk and broke into noisy sobs. Heather cuddled her close, wishing with all her heart that she'd never let herself be drawn into this situation in the first place. What on earth had she been thinking of? All she'd done was upset Grace and upset herself as well.

'I'm sorry, Heather.'

She glanced round when Ross rose to his feet, feeling her heart turn over when she saw the regret on his face. He was several inches taller than she was and she had to tilt back her head to look at him. It made her feel incredibly vulnerable to stand there staring up at him without being able to mask her own feelings properly.

'There's nothing to apologise for. It's my fault for not checking the time,' she replied, deliberately pretending to misunderstand him.

'I'm sorry for having raked up the past when it's obvious that you can't bear to talk about it.' His voice was low but it was clear that he didn't intend to go along with the pretence for politeness's sake.

'I've no idea what you're talking about,' she snapped. 'Thank you for the tea, Mr Tanner. Now, if you'll excuse me…'

She went to brush past him, feeling her breath catch when he put his hand on her arm and stopped her. Even through the thickness of her fleece jacket she could feel the heat from his fingers burning her skin.

'If you ever need to talk, Heather—' he began, but she didn't let him finish, couldn't when she knew that she just might be tempted to pour out the whole dreadful story to him. The thought of how she would feel afterwards was more than she could cope with.

'I won't!'

She shrugged off his hand and he didn't try to detain her again as she hurried to the door. There were a lot of people milling around outside the café but Heather didn't stop as she made for the path that would take her home. Grace was still sobbing but she quietened after a few minutes and soon fell asleep on Heather's shoulder.

Heather slowed down, realising it was unlikely that Ross would follow her. She must have made it perfectly clear that she'd wanted to get away from him. She sighed because it wasn't like her to overreact like that. It had never happened before so what was it about Ross Tanner that made it so difficult for her to remain in control?

She tried to work it out but it was impossible. The only thing she could do was ensure that she never placed herself in such a difficult position again. The last thing she needed was her life being turned upside down when she'd finally achieved a degree of calm after all the turmoil. She would make it clear to Ross that she wasn't interested in him playing any part in her life....

Her heart lurched when it struck her that she'd already accepted she would see him again. He wasn't the type of man who would be put off by what had happened that day when he was obviously determined to get to know her better. Melanie had been right—Ross *was* attracted to her.

Heather took a deep breath but there was no way that she could pretend the idea didn't make her feel all warm and tingly inside. She might not want Ross prying into her past, might not want him in her future either, but she couldn't claim to be *indifferent* to him.

Ross took the twins home after they had tired themselves out. He was bitterly aware that he'd made a complete mess of things with Heather. He shouldn't have tried to press her into telling him about her past. He should have waited until she'd been ready to tell him of her own accord.

He sighed as he let the boys into the house. The chances of Heather ever being ready to tell him her deepest secrets were non-existent. Why should he imagine that she would want to bare her soul to him? Just because he felt this...*connection* to her didn't mean that she reciprocated.

The thought made Ross feel even more dejected and Kate—with all the astuteness of a sibling—quickly picked up on his mood. Shooing the twins into the playroom to watch a cartoon, she sat down to grill him.

'So why are you looking so glum, big brother? And before you try to deny it, I have to say that you don't look your usual laid-back self. Is it woman trouble, by any chance?' she demanded, easing herself onto the sofa.

'What makes you think that?' he hedged. 'I could be having problems at work or trouble with my flat—anything, in fact.'

'You could but you're not.' She grinned at him. 'Come on, Ross, I know you too well. Nothing ever affects you. That isn't meant as a criticism. I think it goes with the job you do. When you're faced with some of the awful situations that you have to deal with then normal, everyday worries must seem very insignificant.'

'Mmm, I suppose you're right. I never really thought about it that way before,' he conceded. 'Obviously, the four years you spent at university weren't a complete waste of time after all!'

He ducked when Kate threw a cushion at him by way of reply. He picked it up and put it back on the sofa, thinking how tired she looked despite the fact that she'd spent the morning resting. He made a note to phone his brother-in-law and see if Mike could come home sooner than planned then sighed when he realised that Kate wasn't going to let the matter drop.

'You can insult me all you like but I'm not letting myself get sidetracked, if that's what you're hoping.' Kate settled back again and smiled angelically. 'So come on, out with it. Who is she and why is she causing you a headache?'

'Her name is Heather Cooper, *Dr* Cooper, to be precise. She's the senior registrar in St Gertrude's A and E department,' he explained wearily, knowing it was pointless trying to hold out. Kate was relentless when it came to ferreting out information. Anyway, maybe it would help to talk through the situation and get her opinion about what he should do.

'I see. Do I take it that she's the lady who ministered to you during your recent stay there? Soothed your fevered brow and all that?' Kate chuckled. She was obviously enjoying herself immensely. 'Don't tell me that your eyes met across a bedpan and—bingo—it was love at first sight?'

'Hardly,' he said dryly, although the memory of how he'd felt when he'd first seen Heather wasn't easily dismissed. He couldn't remember ever reacting so strongly to anyone before. He cleared his throat, somewhat uncomfortable with the idea.

'Heather doesn't dole out bedpans for a start. She's far too important for that.'

'Oh, pardon me! Anyway, you're just splitting hairs because

you're too embarrassed to admit that you've fallen for the lovely doctor. Am I right or am I right?'

Ross rolled his eyes. 'You've been reading too many romantic novels. Pity help poor Mike when he gets home!'

He held up his hand when his sister went to butt in because he didn't want her prising too much out of him. Admitting that he was attracted to Heather was one thing but he wasn't prepared to go any further than that.

His stomach lurched because the thought that it might be more than just physical attraction was alarming. He knew so little about Heather that it would be foolish to imagine even for a nanosecond that he might have fallen in love with her. He'd never believed in the theory of love at first sight and wasn't about to subscribe to it now. However, the idea prickled at the back of his mind like a thorn.

'Heather is a very attractive woman and I admit that I'm interested in her. The problem is that she doesn't seem the least bit interested in me.'

'That must have been a blow to the old ego! No wonder it's whetted your appetite, Ross. I might be your sister but I'm well aware there aren't *that* many women in the world who would turn you down.'

Ross frowned as he considered what Kate had said, or the first bit of it at least. Was it Heather's lack of interest that had, perversely, aroused his?

'Have you tried asking her out?'

He looked up when his sister spoke, undecided if that was the real explanation as to why he was so drawn to Heather. 'Yes. I invited her out for dinner and she turned me down flat.'

'Maybe she's already seeing someone,' Kate suggested. 'Or perhaps she's having to work long hours. The papers are always going on about the shortage of staff in our hospitals and A and E departments are reportedly the hardest hit of all.'

'I suppose either is possible,' he admitted gruffly, although it grieved him to have to add another man to the equation. Maybe Heather wanted to spend any free time she had with Carlisle? He hurried on before the idea could take root.

'She has a child, a little girl who looks to be about two years old, so she can't have much spare time, I don't imagine.'

'Not if she's working full-time and looking after a child,' Kate agreed. 'What about the child's father? Is he no longer on the scene?'

'Heather told me that he'd died before her daughter was born.'

'Oh, how sad! It must have been really hard for her,' Kate exclaimed sympathetically.

'It must. Oddly enough, I sensed there was some tragedy in her past when we first met.' He sighed when Kate looked at him quizzically. 'I come across a lot of people in my job who have suffered and I recognised the signs.'

'Which makes you ideally placed to understand what she's been through,' Kate suggested.

'Maybe. The problem is that she seems reluctant to talk about what happened.'

'Maybe she needs to get to know you better before she opens up.'

'You could be right.' Ross frowned. Was the explanation as simple as that? After all, Heather didn't really know him so why should he expect her to open her heart and tell him all about herself?

The twins came back just then to tell Kate that the video had finished and they were hungry. Ross stood up. 'OK, guys, I'll make you something to eat. Let your mum have a rest.'

He herded the boys to the door, glancing round when Kate said, 'Thanks, Ross. I can't wait till I'm back to my normal self. All this sitting around is driving me crazy.'

'Enjoy it while you can. You'll have no time to lounge around once junior arrives. Anyway, it gives me a chance to get in some practice at being the perfect uncle.'

'Oh, you're pretty good at that already.' Kate winked at him. 'You need to work on your parenting skills so you'll be ready for fatherhood. That's your next big test.'

'I need to find the right woman first,' he pointed out dryly.

'Maybe you already have,' Kate said innocently.

Ross didn't say anything as he left the room. He took a deep breath but the image that swam before his eyes made his blood heat. Heather would look even more beautiful pregnant with his child.

He groaned out loud. He had to get a grip before this got completely out of hand! Maybe he *was* attracted to Heather and maybe he *did* want to get to know her better, but he wasn't planning on marrying her.

Another picture swiftly formed in his mind's eye and his hands clenched. Now he could see Heather walking down the aisle, looking an absolute vision in white lace. She had flowers in her hair and the most radiant smile on her face....

Ross sucked in air like a drowning man and the image faded, but he was shaking as he went into the kitchen and set about making the twins some lunch. He wasn't sure what was happening to him but he had to find a way to take control of himself. He couldn't keep letting thoughts of Heather rule his life like they had been doing. If Heather wasn't interested in him then there were other women who were. He would make a few phone calls when he got home, kick-start his social life, and forget about Heather Cooper.

It was only as he was spooning baked beans onto slices of toast that he remembered his forthcoming visit to St Gertrude's. Whether he liked it or not, he would have to see Heather one last time but he would play it cool. He would stick strictly to the reason for his visit and be polite but aloof....

And pigs might fly, a small inner voice taunted. Remaining aloof around Heather was asking the impossible!

CHAPTER FOUR

'TIME of death, four thirty-two. Thanks, everyone. We gave it our best shot.'

Heather peeled off her latex gloves and tossed them into the waste sack. Her blood-spattered plastic apron quickly followed. The patient, a forty-five-year-old man called Dennis Watson, had been mending a loose chimney pot when he had slipped and fallen through the glass roof of a conservatory. He had suffered multiple lacerations, including damage to his femoral artery. Although the A and E team had done all they could, he had bled to death before they could get him to Theatre.

Resus looked like a scene from a horror film with pools of blood all over the floor and all the staff liberally spattered with it. Just for a second Heather found herself wondering why on earth she did such a job before she caught sight of Rob Bryce, their new houseman. He looked so shocked by what he'd just witnessed that she immediately forgot about herself and went to have a word with him.

'Are you OK, Rob?' she asked, drawing him aside as Melanie began to clear up the bloodied dressings they'd used. The cleaning crew would need to be called in and she mentally crossed her fingers that they wouldn't have another full-blown emergency until the room was fit to be used again.

'I'm fine,' Rob replied quickly. However, Heather could tell that he was only saying what he thought she wanted to hear.

Glancing over her shoulder, she mouthed to Mel that she was taking Rob to the staffroom and got a thumbs-up in reply. The rest of the team had obviously realised how stressful the incident had been for the young trainee. They'd all been new to the job at one time and could remember how they'd felt in the early days.

'Let's have a cup of tea,' Heather suggested, leading the way. She smiled at Rob. 'The first rule when working in A and E is never to miss out on the chance of a cup of tea because it might be hours before you get another one!'

'I must remember that.'

Rob managed a weak smile as he followed her into the corridor. There were only a few people waiting in Reception so Heather was confident that Ben could hold the fort a while longer. He'd returned to work the previous day, claiming that he was fully recovered from his illness, although he still looked a bit under the weather.

She made a note to have a word with him then sighed. She had to sort out Rob instead of getting sidetracked. It wasn't the first time that she'd found her concentration wavering that week either. Ever since Saturday, she'd found her mind skipping off at tangents all the time. It was alarming when she was normally so focused, doubly so when she suspected that it was a repercussion from her meeting with Ross Tanner. What was it about the man that disturbed her so much?

There was still no answer to that question so once again she pushed it to the back of her mind as they entered the staffroom. There was nobody else in there so she shut the door and went to plug in the kettle. Rob looked very ill at ease, as though he was worried that he might be in for a telling-off, so she hurried to reassure him.

'That was a really nasty incident we had to deal with. Watching someone bleeding to death in front of you has to be one of the most traumatic experiences you can go through.'

'It upset you as well? I didn't think it would....' Rob broke off, obviously fearing that he might have said the wrong thing.

'Because I've been doing this job for some time?' Heather sighed. 'I'm afraid it doesn't work like that. It still gets to you but you learn to deal with it. You have to because you have to think about the next patient who's going to need your help.'

'I know you're right, but when I saw all that blood...' Rob gulped and suddenly sat down.

Heather dropped tea-bags into the pot while she gave him a

moment to compose himself. She made the tea and poured them both a mug, adding a spoonful of sugar to Rob's. Carrying the mugs over to the table, she sat down and tried not to think about how Ross had done the same thing for her on Saturday. He'd tried to help her get over the shock she'd had by plying her with tea and sympathy.

Heat fizzed through her veins as she recalled the concern in his eyes when he had looked at her. It was as though her mind had captured the moment and held fast to it. But, then, there were so many other images that had crowded into her head at odd moments this past week, like how tall Ross was, how good-looking, how caring he'd been towards his nephews and Grace…

'I'd no idea what five litres of blood really looked like. It was absolutely everywhere! And as fast as we tried to pump more in, out it came. That's something they don't tell you about in med school.'

Heather blinked and the room rushed back into focus. She put her mug on the table and took a deep breath. She had to stop thinking about Ross all the time. She'd allowed herself quite enough leeway since Saturday.

'Unfortunately, nothing you learn from a textbook can ever prepare you for the reality of doing this job, Rob,' she said gently. 'You'll have to deal with a lot of very unpleasant things but it's all part and parcel of it, I'm afraid.'

'And what if you can't deal with them?' Rob ran his hands through his short ginger hair. Heather could see how worried he looked. 'Does it mean you're not cut out for medicine?'

'Not necessarily. It could be that you just aren't cut out for accident and emergency work.'

Heather bit back a sigh because the last thing she wanted was for Rob to be so disheartened by what he'd witnessed that he gave up medicine all together. He wouldn't be the first young doctor who suddenly realised the job wasn't what he'd hoped it would be, but it would be a shame to lose him.

'Look, Rob, what happened today was exceptional even by our standards, and you acquitted yourself extremely well.' She shrugged when he looked at her uncertainly. 'The reason we don't usually accept housemen straight from med school is because they need to get some idea of the problems they'll encounter. You've been thrown in at the deep end and the last thing I want is for you to be put off by this. If you want me to arrange a transfer for you to a different department then I'll do so.'

'No-o,' Rob said slowly. 'It would feel as though I'd given up before I'd had a real shot at the job. I think I'd always regret it if I did that.'

'Are you sure?' Heather gave him a moment to reconsider her offer then smiled when he nodded. 'Good for you! I have a feeling that you'll make a first-rate doctor, Rob. Just don't expect too much of yourself too soon.'

'Thanks.' He smiled back, looking so much happier that Heather knew she'd been right to talk to him. Sometimes all it needed was to talk through your feelings and sort things out before a problem arose.

Her pulse leapt as she was forced to admit that she had never followed that advice herself. She had refused to talk about her feelings after Stewart had died. Even to her mother she'd had difficulty explaining the depth of her despair. Maybe she should take Ross up on his offer and pour out the whole story to him?

She was so stunned by the idea that she didn't hear the door opening, and jumped when Melanie appeared at her side.

'You look lost in thought, Heather. Hope it's a nice one about a tall, dark, handsome fireman,' the young nurse teased before she suddenly sobered. 'Anyway, Mr Watson's wife has arrived. I've put her in the relatives' room and told her that you'll be in to see her shortly.'

'Thanks, Mel.' Heather stood up, grateful that she'd been spared having to think up a reply to that remark about Ross Tanner. The fact that she *had* been thinking about him didn't sit easily with her.

She looked round when Rob got to his feet as well and shook her head. 'You can stay here and finish your tea if you like.'

'No, it's OK. I'd rather get back to work.' He took a deep breath. 'Do you want me to come with you to see Mrs Watson?'

'No, it's fine,' she assured him, although she admired him for offering. 'Maybe you could give Ben a hand. If we can clear the backlog then we'll be ready if we get another emergency.'

Rob hurried off, trying to hide his relief at being spared the ordeal of telling the man's wife that her husband had died. Heather turned to Mel with a satisfied smile. 'I think he'll make it, don't you?'

'I hope so. We're short-handed enough as it is. I don't know how they expect us to cope when we've got so many vacancies. Have they found anyone for the consultant's post yet, do you know?'

'The last I heard they were going to re-advertise it,' Heather explained. 'None of the previous candidates were suitably qualified.'

'Looks as though you'll have to carry on doing that job as well as your own for a bit longer,' Mel said sympathetically.

They left the staffroom and Heather paused in the corridor. 'I'll go and break the news to Mrs Watson. Do you think you could find a porter to help you move Mr Watson to the treatment room? I expect Mrs Watson will want to see him and I really don't want her going near Resus at the moment with the state it's in.'

'Will do.'

Melanie hurried away while Heather made her way to the relatives' room. This was the part of the job she hated most, but it had to be done. All she could do was try to make it as easy as possible for the poor woman, but she knew from personal experience how traumatic it would be for Dennis Watson's wife.

'Dr Cooper!'

Heather looked round when she heard someone calling her and saw Norma Pierce, the chief executive's secretary, hurrying towards her. 'Did you want me, Mrs Pierce?'

'Yes. I'm afraid there's been a bit of mix-up somewhere along the line,' the elegant, grey-haired woman explained, handing Heather a sheet of paper. 'You should have received notification of this visit last week but for some reason the letters got sent to my office instead of being distributed to each department. I've been away on holiday and only just found them.'

'Thank you.'

Heather unfolded the letter as the other woman hurried away. It was an official notification to say that the hospital would be inspected the following day prior to the issuing of a new fire safety certificate. Heather made a note to tell everyone and started to fold up the letter when a name typed on it seemed to jump right out at her. The inspection was being carried out by a team led by Station Officer Ross Tanner.

The words swam before her eyes. Ross would be right here in the hospital tomorrow morning at ten o'clock and there was no way she could avoid him.

Ross parked his car in one of the slots designated for official visitors. Reaching over, he took his hat off the back seat and brushed a few specks of dust off it. He must have carried out umpteen safety checks during his time with the brigade but that day he felt as nervous as a rookie. His stomach was churning and his palms were actually damp. It was proof of the effect Heather had on him and just for a moment he regretted ever formulating this plan before common sense asserted itself. The hospital was due for an inspection and he had a job to do first and foremost. Everything else had to come second to that.

He got out of the car and looked round to see if Terry Green and Jack Marsh had arrived. As station officer, Ross had to be available if there was a problem back at the station so they had come in separate cars. He spotted the men crossing the car park and waited for them.

'Right, you both know the drill. We'll start on the ground floor and work our way up through the building,' he explained as they headed towards the hospital's main entrance. 'I've brought copies of the building plans for each of us so we can each take a department to save time.'

He distributed the plans then went to the reception desk to check in. The receptionist had been warned about their visit and had passes all ready for them. Ross clipped the plastic-covered visitor's permit to the lapel of his uniform jacket then turned to the other two men.

'Terry, you take Outpatients and, Jack, you can have the physiotherapy department. The name of each departmental head who you'll need to liaise with is on your check-sheets.'

'Where are you off to?' Jack checked his copy of the floor plans. 'A and E, is it? It's the only other department on the ground floor.'

'Yes,' Ross agreed tersely, wondering if he should ask one of the others to swop with him. Heather must know about his visit and he couldn't help wondering how she felt about it. Did she suspect that he had engineered it initially so that he could see her?

'Rather you than me,' Jack said cheerfully. 'I'm not all that fond of the sight of blood. I take it that we can't use our radios?'

'No. They could interfere with some of the equipment. Ask the reception staff to page me when you're done and we'll go from there.'

Both men nodded and went their separate ways. Ross took a deep breath then strode along the corridor that led to the accident and emergency department. It was busy that morning so he joined the queue at the reception desk and introduced himself to the middle-aged receptionist when it was his turn.

'Oh, hi! Heather warned us that we were due an inspection this morning.' The woman, whose name badge identified her as Trish, leant over the desk and looked around. 'I'm not sure where she's got to.… Mel, have you seen Heather?'

A young, blond nurse, whom Ross remembered from when he'd been admitted, paused on her way to the cubicles. She laughed when she saw Ross. 'Back again so soon, Mr Tanner? We'll be putting you on the coffee-making rota next!'

Ross summoned a smile, wondering if there'd been more to that comment than just a friendly greeting. Had Heather told the staff about his last visit, when he'd asked her out?

He tried to dismiss the idea as being of very little importance but he hated to think that she might have laughed about it with the staff. 'Not when you taste my coffee. The guys at the station refuse to drink it.'

'Oh, well, you can't be good at everything is what I always say,' the nurse observed cheerfully. 'Anyway, I'll tell Heather you're here. Won't be a sec.'

She disappeared and Ross moved aside so that he wasn't blocking the desk. He looked around the waiting room, sighing when he saw the state of some of the people who were in there that day. It never failed to amaze him how much damage folk managed to inflict on themselves.

'Station Officer Tanner?'

He nearly jumped out of his skin when he heard Heather's voice. He swung round and felt his heart begin to race when he saw her. Her hair was coiled into its customary no-nonsense knot and she wasn't wearing a scrap of make-up, but she looked so heart-breakingly lovely that his insides spasmed with desire. He wanted to sweep her into his arms right there in the middle of the department, kiss her until she clung helplessly to him then kiss her all over again but tenderly and gently this time as he promised her undying devotion.

His muscles contracted until he was in genuine agony. If that wasn't love then what the hell was it?

Heather swallowed but the lump in her throat wouldn't budge. She'd been mentally preparing herself for seeing Ross ever since she'd arrived at work that morning, but the polite little speech she had rehearsed had completely dried up. It was the way he was looking at her, his hazel eyes filled with such warmth that it seemed to melt her very bones. For the first time since Stewart had died, Heather experienced the heady tug of physical desire.

Her response shocked her so much that she recoiled and

cannoned into Rob, who happened to be passing along the corridor. They were both thrown off balance by the collision and there was a scuffle as they tried to right themselves.

'Careful!' Ross caught hold of her arm and steadied her.

'Thanks.' Heather hurriedly withdrew her arm. She apologised to Rob but her heart was racing. It took every scrap of courage she possessed to face Ross as the young houseman went on his way.

'That was clumsy of me. I must be more careful what I'm doing in future.' She summoned a smile but it wasn't easy to pretend that nothing had happened. She'd always thought that part of her had died with Stewart, but she'd been wrong, it seemed.

'Accidents happen, not that I need to tell you that.'

Ross treated her to a wry smile as he looked around the waiting room. Heather felt the drumming beat of her heart gradually subside when she realised he had no idea what had really happened. It was difficult to hide her relief but she knew it would be a mistake to let Ross see there was anything wrong with her.

'You certainly don't. Anyway, we'd better not waste any more time. I expect you're as busy as we are. Where do you want to start?'

'Storerooms first then we'll work through the department, checking for any obvious hazards,' he explained. 'St Gertrude's has an excellent safety record so I'm not anticipating any major problems.'

'The health and safety officer is very keen and does regular spot checks.' She led the way to the first of the storerooms and unlocked the door, determined to keep things on a purely professional footing. 'Heaven help any department that doesn't come up to scratch. You end up being bombarded with paperwork!'

'Better than having staff and patients injured,' he observed, looking around. 'It's amazing how many people don't realise the dangers of storing flammable items next to power points, for instance. They don't understand that an electrical spark can cause a fire.'

'Sometimes it's a case of familiarity breeding contempt,' she suggested as he made a note on one of the sheets attached to his clipboard. 'People get so used to handling flammable substances that they forget about the dangers.'

'That's very true.' Ross followed her to the next storeroom. 'Take that fire I attended the other week—the one where that little boy was injured. That was caused by a tenant from one of the flats using glue to mend a picture frame. He ignored the warning on the tin about it being highly flammable and lit the gas cooker. The vapour from the glue ignited and the whole place went up.'

'How awful!' Heather shuddered. She glanced around the room, trying not to think about how close Ross had come to losing his life that day. It was too much to deal with after what had happened to Stewart, although it surprised her that she should equate the two events.

'A moment's carelessness is all it takes.' Ross crouched down to check the labels on some plastic containers.

Heather felt her breath catch when she saw the muscles in his thighs bunch. He leant forward to reach one of the containers at the back and she bit her lip when she saw how the action had made his uniform jacket strain across his powerful shoulders. All of a sudden it felt as though she was seeing him properly for the very first time and she found that she couldn't drag her gaze away.

His body was the classically perfect male shape with wide shoulders and a broad chest tapering down to a trim waist and hips. Those long, muscular legs gave him the advantage of an above average height, somewhere in the region of six feet two, she'd guess. When he stood up to check some items stacked on a shelf, Heather's eyes followed and took fascinated stock of the crisp, dark brown hair and strongly marked brows, the high cheekbones and firm jaw, the commanding slope of his nose. All in all, Ross was an extremely handsome man, she concluded, and he certainly wouldn't pass unnoticed in a crowd.

'This container is leaking. It needs to be replaced.'

He looked round and Heather hastily averted her gaze, but it alarmed her that she should have been standing there admiring him. She couldn't afford to let herself be attracted to Ross. She had to remember what he did for a living. She'd been through enough heartache for one lifetime.

'Heather, are you all right?'

The concern in his voice finally penetrated her thoughts and she rallied. 'Sorry. You said the container was leaking?'

'Yes. It needs removing and the spillage cleaning up. Everything else is fine but I'd suggest that you have someone check all the containers to be on the safe side.'

He put out a restraining hand when she turned to leave the room. 'Are you sure you're feeling all right? You looked a bit…well…lost is the only word I can think of.'

'I'm fine.' She managed to smile but it was unnerving to realise how easily he seemed to pick up on her moods. She hunted for an explanation that would stop him asking any more questions. However, the fact that she'd felt it necessary to remind herself about the dangers of getting involved with him really worried her.

'Grace had rather a restless night and I didn't get much sleep. I'm a bit spaced out this morning.'

'It can't be easy, looking after her as well as working full time,' he observed quietly.

'My mother helps. I certainly wouldn't be able to manage without her.'

She glanced down, feeling a shiver run through as she saw how his fingers were curled around her arm. His hands were well shaped with long fingers and broad palms, but they were the hands of a man who didn't shy away from hard physical work. It made her wonder how they would feel on her bare skin, if his fingers would be slightly rough to the touch.

Her breathing quickened as her mind captured the idea and ran riot with it. How wonderful it would be to feel the abrasion of his fingertips caressing her naked body. She could imagine the delicious friction they would create as they moved over her skin—travelling up her thighs, cresting the curves of her hips and dipping into the hollow of her waist before they finally arrived at the fullness of her breasts....

The shrill peel of the emergency telephone made her jump. Heather raised startled grey eyes to the hazel ones which were watching her so intently. 'I...I'd better go and see what's happened,' she said haltingly, finding it incredibly hard to force out any words when she desperately needed to draw in oxygen.

'Of course.'

Ross's response was only what she would have expected, but the tone of his voice imbued the words with all kinds of meanings. Heather felt the colour ebb and flow in her face and could do nothing about it as she continued to stare into his eyes. Had Ross guessed what she'd been thinking just now?

The rational side of her mind said, no, of course not, that it simply wasn't possible to read someone else's thoughts. However, the look in his eyes said that it was true. Every caress she'd imagined he had shared with her, mentally if not physically, at least.

The idea was so overwhelming that Heather couldn't move. It was Ross who broke away when his pager beeped. He checked the display and frowned.

'Urgent message from the station. Can I use your phone?'

Heather jumped like someone being awoken from a trance. 'Of course. You can use the one in the office. It will be a bit more private in there.' She quickly led the way to the office and opened the door. 'I'll leave you to it while I see what's going on.'

'Thanks.'

He hurried into the room and went straight to the phone. Heather willed herself to calm down as she went to the desk, but she must have looked a bit odd because she saw Trish staring at her. Abby McLeod was talking on the emergency telephone and furiously jotting down notes at the same time.

'Are you OK, Heather?' Trish demanded. She had a ten-

dency to mother the rest of the staff, and whilst normally
Heather appreciated the receptionist's kindness she would have
preferred not to be on the receiving end that day. 'You don't
look so good, I must say. I hope you've not caught Ben's bug.'

'Let's hope not.' Fortunately, Abby hung up just then so
Heather was spared having to think up anything else to say. It
was obvious from the sister's expression that they had a major
incident on their hands.

'There's been an explosion at that new dockside complex
they're building,' Abby informed her. 'Ambulance Control
have been told to expect multiple casualties so they've des-
patched six crews to the scene. They've asked us to send a
rapid response team because we're the nearest. Apparently,
there's a huge tailback of traffic because of the smoke drifting
across the road so we're having to use the helicopter. It will
be here in roughly five minutes' time to collect us.'

'Right.' Heather thought rapidly then began to issue instructions. 'You and I will attend the accident, Abby. That will leave
Ben, Rob and Mel here. Janet and Doreen are due in at twelve
but if you could phone the nursing manager, Trish, and ask her
if there's any spare staff, that would be a help.'

She didn't wait for Trish to reply as she led the way to the
storeroom where they kept everything they needed for an incident like this. Several of the main London hospitals had been
equipped to provide rapid response teams, although St
Gertrude's had been one of the last to join the scheme. Heather
had been called upon only twice in the few months they had
been providing the service and she wanted to be certain that
she had everything they would need.

She checked the ready-packed cases of medical supplies
while Abby sorted out the clothing they would need to wear.
Waterproof jackets and trousers adorned with fluorescent green
stripes identifying them as medical personnel were stocked in
various sizes. Abby quickly got kitted up then passed Heather
a jacket and trousers, waiting until she'd dragged them on over
her clothes before handing her a safety helmet as well.

'Thanks.' Heather rammed the helmet onto her head but

didn't waste time fastening the strap under her chin. The helicopter would be on its way by now and she didn't want to keep
it waiting. She snatched up one of the medical kits, passed
another to Abby and turned to leave, then stopped dead. Ross
was standing in the doorway and the sight of him seemed to
have drained all the strength from her limbs.

She didn't notice when Abby excused herself and left. Her
heart was thumping too loudly to hear anything. Ross took a
couple of steps and it seemed as though everything was happening in slow motion as he came towards her.

'I've been called back to the station. There's been an explosion at that new dockside complex,' he said softly, his eyes
tracing her face in a way that made Heather feel so weak that
it was an effort to remain upright.

'I know.' She had to wet her lips because they seemed to
be sticking together. 'Th-that's where I'm going. We've been
asked to send a rapid response team.'

'It will be dangerous, Heather. That area of the docks was
used for storing crude oil. The tanks were drained years ago
but it appears one of them must have been leaking. There's a
lake of oil underneath it which has caught fire.'

He took hold of the strap on her helmet and fastened it securely under her chin. Heather closed her eyes when she felt
his fingers brushing the soft skin beneath her jaw because the
touch of them was every bit as sensual as she'd imagined it
would be. 'Make sure you keep that on at all times.'

'I will.'

Her voice was little more than a whisper but there was no
disguising the wealth of emotions it held. Heather felt her heart
jerk when she heard Ross swallow. His fingers slid along her
jaw, tracing its delicate curve, before they began exploring her
face.

Heather could feel a moan of pleasure building inside her as
she felt the delicious friction he was creating wherever his fingers touched her, but before it could emerge his hand returned
to her chin. Time seemed to come to a standstill when she felt

him tilt up her face so that his mouth could claim hers in a kiss which was so gentle that she wondered if she'd dreamt it.

Her eyes flew open but Ross had already moved away. He paused in the doorway and Heather felt as though she was being enveloped in a great sea of warmth when he smiled at her.

'Take care, Heather.'

'You, too, Ross,' she whispered, although she wasn't sure if he'd heard her as he hurried away. She went out to the corridor and automatically turned in the direction of the lifts. Conscious thought was beyond her at that moment but she knew that she needed to get up to the helipad on the roof before the helicopter arrived.

Abby was waiting by the lifts so they travelled up together. Heather responded as best she could as the nurse chatted about the type of injuries they might encounter, but it felt as though she was functioning on autopilot. Ross had kissed her as though he really cared about her, but surely that couldn't be true?

The lift arrived at the top floor and they had to get out and use the stairs to reach the roof. There was a locked door to be negotiated first, however, a security measure to prevent patients and visitors gaining access to the roof. Try as she may, Heather couldn't remember the code for it.

'Let me do it.' Abby quickly keyed in the numbers then grinned at her. 'Nice to know you're as susceptible as the rest of us are, Heather.'

'Sorry?' Heather pushed open the door, holding onto it as the wind threatened to send it crashing back against the wall.

'To the charms of a handsome man, of course. And I have to say that they don't come much more handsome than Station Officer Tanner!'

Abby laughed but Heather was hard-pressed to hide her dismay. If people were starting to notice her reaction to Ross then the situation really was becoming serious.

She closed the door with hands that were no longer steady. She could try to ignore the effect Ross had on her but that was like putting a dressing over a festering wound: it wasn't really *dealing* with the problem. She had to excise him from her mind—and her life—once and for all.

'Here we go!'

She turned when she heard Abby shouting to tell her the helicopter was in sight. They both huddled against the wall as it set down neatly on the landing pad. The down draught from the rotor blades was tremendous as they hurried to board it. One of the crew gave Abby a hand and hauled her on board, then helped Heather, too. They strapped themselves in as the helicopter took off again. It circled the hospital then turned towards the river. Rooftops passed beneath them in a blur and the noise was deafening. It all added to the sense of confusion Heather felt, the feeling that her life was racing out of control.

She took a deep breath. She mustn't let that happen. She couldn't! No matter how she felt about Ross or how he felt about her, she had to put a stop to what was happening.

Tears stung her eyes and she turned to stare out of the window because, crazy as it sounded, she knew how hard it was going to be. There was something about Ross that filled all the empty spaces in her life, but that kind of happiness came at too big a cost. She'd loved one hero and she wouldn't make the mistake of falling in love with another.

CHAPTER FIVE

'I WANT you to get the roof off that van as fast as possible. We need to get those people out of there. We're barely managing to contain the blaze as it is. The whole lot could go up again at any minute and they're directly in the firing line.'

Ross looked around as the men hurried away to carry out his orders. The crew from Hexton had been first on the scene, although he'd been assured they would be receiving back-up very shortly. Two neighbouring fire stations were sending pump engines, along with a variety of specialised cutting and lifting gear.

The explosion had gouged a huge hole out of the ground. Thick plumes of black smoke and flames were billowing from it and the air was redolent with the smell of burning oil. The three men who'd been dismantling the fuel tank were still unaccounted for, but it seemed unlikely that anyone could have survived the explosion let alone the subsequent blaze.

The blast had also caved in the front wall of one of the warehouses surrounding the dock. The building was in the process of being converted into luxury flats and nobody seemed to know how many men had been working inside it at the time. So far Ross hadn't been able to put a figure on the number of casualties they needed to look for. There could be two or two dozen men trapped inside the building for all he knew.

His mouth compressed as he strode across the rubble-strewn ground to speak to the site manager again. The man had been extremely evasive about the number of people employed on the site. Ross suspected that a lot of them would be migrant workers who weren't listed in any official records. It helped to cut costs when there was no insurance to be paid for workers who officially didn't exist. However, it made his job all the more difficult if he didn't know exactly how many people were missing.

'A word please, Mr Bradburn,' he said shortly, tapping the man on the shoulder. Ray Bradburn had spent all his time on his mobile phone since Ross had arrived and he didn't look pleased about being interrupted now. However, he obviously decided it would be a mistake not to co-operate when he saw the expression on Ross's face.

'How can I help you, Station Officer Tanner?' he said, making an effort to be polite as he cut short his call.

'You can help by telling me exactly how many men you had working inside that warehouse.' Ross didn't bother wasting time on pleasantries. He had a job to do and that was the only thing that mattered, apart from making sure Heather was safe, of course.

His heart knocked painfully against his ribs when he looked round and failed to spot her. She'd already been attending to the injured by the time he'd arrived on the scene. They'd not had chance to exchange more than a couple of words in passing but he'd made sure he'd known where she was at any given time. The situation was extremely volatile and he didn't want to run the risk of her being in the wrong place if there was another explosion.

It was hard to contain his impatience when he was so afraid that she might have placed herself in danger. He held up his hand when Bradburn started to bluster about it being difficult to give him an accurate figure.

'Health and safety regulations state that employers must maintain a record of all the people working for them. You must have a system for signing in each day.'

'Um, yes, of course.' Bradburn ran a finger around his collar. He looked decidedly uneasy about having to answer the question. 'But not all the men remember to sign the daily work sheets, you understand.'

'I do.' Ross sighed wearily. This could take for ever if he didn't make it clear that he wasn't prepared to waste any more time. 'Let's stop fencing with words, Mr Bradburn. Frankly,

I'm not interested in your business methods. You wouldn't be the first person who pays workers cash in hand and doesn't keep records. I need to know how many men are inside that building.'

'Seven.' Bradburn seemed to slump as he realised there was no point prevaricating. 'Two company employees plus five casual labourers—Armenians or something. I'm not sure exactly because they don't speak much English.'

'And that's the lot?' Ross fixed him with a steely-eyed stare. 'You're absolutely sure about that?'

'Yes. Look, there's no need to say anything about this to the authorities, is there?' Bradburn gave him an ingratiating smile. 'You're a man of the world and you understand how these things work. On a project like this you have to trim the costs wherever you can....'

Ross didn't bother hearing him out. He wasn't interested. The fact that Bradburn had been prepared to risk people's lives rather than own up to what he'd been doing filled him with disgust.

He went to get the rescue operation organised. Fortunately, the rest of the fire crews had arrived now. There were also a number of ambulances parked nearby and he could see some paramedics loading the first of the injured on board. However, try as he may, he still couldn't see any sign of Heather.

It was hard to contain his fear that something had happened to her, but Ross was aware that he had a job to do. As the senior officer there that day, he was in charge of the fire ground and it was his duty to deploy the crews where they would be needed most.

He quickly informed his colleagues that there were seven men still inside the warehouse and another three unaccounted for. The crew from Rosedale fire station had brought lifting gear with them so it was decided that they would remove the rubble that was blocking the entrance to the warehouse. The other crew would join the men from Hexton and try to contain the blaze. There were several yachts moored in the dock basin and there was a danger that they could catch fire, too.

Once Ross was sure that everyone knew what they were doing, he went to find Heather. She'd been tending to some of the injured beside one of the Portakabins when he'd last seen her, but there was no sign of her when he went to check. Ross spotted a nurse he recognised from St Gertrude's and hurried over to see if she knew where Heather had got to.

'She's down there.' The nurse pointed to the slipway leading to the dock. 'They've found one of the men who were working on the tank when it exploded and it seems he's still alive.'

'Thanks,' Ross said gratefully, barely able to contain his relief. He ran to the slipway and immediately spotted Heather among the group of people gathered down by the water. He hurried towards her, pausing briefly when the crowd parted to let him through and he saw the condition of the young man she was attending to.

The poor fellow was covered in oil from head to toe and the few places where it hadn't stuck to him, Ross could see that his skin had been burned away. Amazingly, he was conscious and Ross could hear Heather talking to him while she attempted to insert a cannula into a vein in his left arm. She looked round when Ross crouched beside her and he could see the sorrow in her eyes.

'How's he doing?' he asked softly, although he suspected that he already knew the answer to that question. With burns of this severity it was unlikely the young man would survive. Heather obviously knew that but there was nothing but confidence in her voice when she replied.

'You're doing fine, aren't you, Andy?' She smiled at the young man. 'You've had something for the pain and you're feeling a lot better now.'

'Much.' The young man could barely speak because of his injuries but it was obvious that he'd been reassured by Heather's upbeat manner. Ross was suddenly filled with admiration for the way she was handling the incident. She was determined to give the poor lad hope, even though Ross could tell how much it was costing her to do so.

Under cover of helping her by holding Andy's arm steady

while she inserted the cannula, he brushed the back of her hand with his knuckles, hoping that she would interpret the gesture the way it had been meant. He just wanted her to know that he was there and that he understood. People tended to believe that medical personnel became hardened to the horrific sights they saw, but he knew from his own experiences that it wasn't so. She glanced up and Ross felt his heart fill with warmth when he saw the gratitude in her eyes. It felt like yet another step forward on top of all the others he'd made that day. He wanted to sing for joy, only that would have been inappropriate in the circumstances. Instead, he contented himself with smiling back then wondered how revealing the smile had been when he saw the colour rush to her cheeks. Surely Heather didn't suspect how important she had become to him?

His heart raced at the idea so it was a moment before he realised that she'd spoken. 'Sorry?' he said, cursing himself for getting carried away. If Heather could keep her mind on the job then he must, too.

'I'm having difficulty finding a vein,' she repeated quietly so Andy couldn't hear. 'He's in shock and his circulatory system is shutting down. I'll have to do a cutdown and see if I can find a suitable vein in his ankle. It's imperative that I get some fluids into him.'

'What can I do to help?' Ross offered immediately.

'Find something to put under him while I cut away his trousers,' she instructed, taking a pair of blunt-tipped scissors from her bag. 'There's all sorts of muck around here and I want to avoid the incision getting infected. I also need a blanket to cover him. The water in that dock is freezing and the loss of body heat is exacerbating the problem.'

'Will do.' Ross got up and hurried up the slipway. He ran straight to the nearest ambulance. 'Dr Cooper needs something to put under a patient while she does a cutdown to find a vein. He's badly burned and in shock and she needs a blanket as well to keep him warm.'

'These should do.' The female paramedic handed him a plastic bag containing a fresh sheet then took a thermal blanket off a shelf. She glanced over her shoulder when her colleague shouted from the cab that they were ready to leave. 'Sorry I can't stay and help, but we've got one man who's had a heart attack and another who looks as though he might have a ruptured spleen.'

'It's OK. I understand.' Ross ran back to the slipway as the ambulance roared away. He ripped open the plastic bag and quickly spread the sheet on the ground, taking care not to jolt Andy as he slid it beneath him.

'Thanks.' Heather tossed her oil-soaked gloves aside and picked up the thermal blanket. One side looked like a conventional cover but the other was made of lightweight foil which would provide maximum insulation.

'Help me cover him with this but try to keep it away from his body. We don't want it sticking to any areas of exposed tissue.' She passed Ross one end of the blanket and grinned at Andy. 'We're going to make a kind of tent with this to keep you warm. OK?'

'Uh-huh.' The young man swallowed painfully. 'They gave me…one like that…after I ran the…London Marathon this year. Maybe I'll get…another one…next year.'

'Let's hope so.' Heather maintained her smile but Ross could tell how hard it was for her to remain upbeat. There was little chance of Andy being fit enough to run again next year. If he survived…and it was a very big if at this stage…then he would need months of painful surgery.

Ross helped Heather cover the young man with the blanket. She pulled on a fresh pair of gloves then took what she needed from her bag and laid it on the sheet. Ross was surprised when he saw that she'd cut away both legs of the young man's trousers from just below the knees and removed both his boots. Fortunately, the burning oil hadn't penetrated Andy's heavy work boots so the skin around his ankles was unscathed.

'I might need to have a couple of tries at it.' She swabbed Andy's ankles with antiseptic. 'His veins are collapsing and it's not going to be easy to find one I can use.'

'I see.' Ross nodded his understanding, although it alarmed

him that she'd been able to read his mind with such accuracy. He couldn't help wondering what other of his thoughts she'd correctly interpreted.

It was an effort to dismiss the idea but it was obvious that Heather was anxious to get started. The paramedics were all busy and the nurse he'd spoken to was still attending to her patient. None of the bystanders looked keen to help so it was him or nobody, basically. Maybe it wasn't part of his job but it was a matter of priorities. Heather needed his help and he wasn't about to let her down.

'What do you want me to do?' he demanded, kneeling beside her on the concrete slipway.

'Put on some gloves first. Then I want you to hold Andy's leg steady.' She smiled at the young man. 'You shouldn't feel this because you're loaded up with pain relief, but feel free to yell if you want to.'

Andy mumbled something but it was obvious that his condition was deteriorating. Ross could tell how worried Heather was as she made a swift incision above the young man's right ankle. She quickly cut down to the vein and deftly slid the cannula into place.

'Thank heavens for that!' She attached a line then took the bag of saline from Ross and fitted it in place. Once she'd opened the valve and released the fluid, she began squeezing the bag. 'We need to get this into him as fast as possible.'

Ross could hear the determination in her voice and found himself uttering a silent prayer that the treatment would work. He couldn't bear to imagine how upset Heather would be if Andy didn't make it after all her efforts. In that moment he realised that if he could be granted just one wish, it would be to stop her suffering any more pain. He wanted to protect and cherish her, erase all the unhappiness from her life—past, present and future—and promise her that she would never suffer any heartache again. But how on earth could he make her a promise like that?

'I'd better get a move on,' he said thickly. He cleared his throat but it hurt to admit how tenuous his link to Heather really was. Maybe she hadn't appeared to be upset when he'd kissed her that morning but he would be a fool to read too much into it. One kiss given and received certainly didn't constitute a relationship!

'There are a couple of people trapped in a van and some others inside that warehouse so I can't hang round here any longer,' he informed her curtly, hating to admit what an idiot he was. The problem was, he'd never found himself in this position before. Most of the women he'd dated had been keen to take the relationship further, but Ross had never been tempted to make that kind of commitment until he'd met Heather.

'You should have said so,' Heather said stiffly, obviously misinterpreting the reason for his abruptness. 'I apologise for being a nuisance and delaying you.'

'You aren't a nuisance and I was glad to help,' he assured her, but maybe he hadn't sounded as convincing as he could have done.

He bit back a sigh when he saw her shuttered expression but there was nothing he could do. The fact that he was even *considering* making a permanent commitment to Heather made his head spin. He needed to think seriously about what he was doing, work out what he wanted from Heather, as well as what he wanted to give her.

Did he want to be her friend or her lover? Because that was what it all boiled down to.

Heather knew it was unreasonable to feel hurt but she couldn't help it. She and Ross had seemed to have worked so well together while they'd been attending to Andy. Even though Ross had only basic medical training, he had anticipated her every need. It was rare to develop that kind of instant rapport with anyone but she realised it would be silly to imagine it meant anything. Ross had simply wanted to speed up the proceedings so he could make his escape.

'Thank you for your help,' she said in a tone that made it

clear she didn't expect him to hang around. 'I'll have Andy sent straight to St Gertrude's now that he's stable.'

'I'll tell the paramedics you have a patient ready for transfer.'

'Don't bother. I can sort everything out from here.' She turned to one of the bystanders. 'Could you ask one of the ambulance crews to bring a stretcher down here?' Out of the corner of her eye she saw Ross start to walk up the slipway but she didn't try to stop him. He had more important things to do than worry about *her*. Maybe it was silly but it still hurt to realise it.

It was late afternoon by the time Heather arrived back at St Gertrude's. The fire had been under control when she'd left the dock and the men who'd been trapped inside the warehouse had been rescued. Amazingly, only one of them had been seriously injured. She and Abby had travelled back in the ambulance with him while the rest of the casualties had been ferried to various hospitals throughout the region. Most had suffered only minor cuts and bruises but they would all need to be checked over.

Heather climbed down from the ambulance after Frank Farnell, one of the paramedics, had opened the doors. 'Can you take him straight to Resus, Frank? I'll put a call through to the cardio team and ask them to send someone down to take a look at him.'

'What do you think is wrong with him, Heather?' Jeannie Roberts, the other member of the two-man ambulance crew, lifted one end of the stretcher while Frank took the other.

'If I had to make a guess, I'd say he's suffering from myocardial contusion.' She shot an assessing look at the man on the stretcher. 'He was hit on the chest by a lump of falling masonry so it's very likely his heart has been bruised. He's hypotensive and there are definite signs of arrhythmia—both classic symptoms—but we'll need to run some tests first. Once we've done an electrocardiograph and checked for any cardiac enzyme changes then we'll have a better idea what's wrong with him.'

'I hope that "we" you're referring to doesn't mean you and me.' Abby groaned as she followed them into the building. 'I'm bushed and I don't mind admitting it. All I want at the moment is a cup of tea and a comfy chair!'

'Then your wish shall be granted!' Heather steered the nurse towards the staffroom. She could understand how Abby felt because she was tired, too. It had been a hectic day and the fact that she'd been dealing with a major burns case had simply added to her overall stress levels.

'You've done more than your fair share, Abby, so go and take a break.'

'You must be just as tired as me, Heather,' Abby pointed out. 'You need a break, too.'

'And I'll have one as soon as I've dealt with this patient,' Heather promised. She knew Abby was right but also knew it would be easier if she kept working. She didn't want to have time on her hands to think about how badly burned Andy had been because it would remind her of Stewart. Neither did she want to think about the fact that Ross had resented helping her. Today of all days she couldn't handle the strain on her emotions.

'Well, make sure you do. You know what they say about all work and no play.' Abby winked at her. 'Maybe I should have a word with Station Officer Tanner the next time I see him and tell him that you need saving from yourself. I'm sure he's got some *very* good ideas about how you could better spend your time!'

Heather blushed at the good-natured teasing. 'I don't know why you imagine that Ross Tanner is the least bit interested in what I do!'

'That's because you haven't noticed the way he looks at you.' Abby shook her head. 'Honestly, Heather, you're one in a million. I can't think of a single woman in this entire hospital who wouldn't be flattered if a hunk like Ross Tanner was making sheep's eyes at her, yet you seem to be oblivious to the effect you have on him.'

'Maybe I'm just not interested,' Heather said quickly. She took a deep breath but it was as though the protective layer with which she'd surrounded herself these past three years or so had suddenly disappeared and her emotions were bubbling up inside her.

How would it feel to have another man love her as Stewart had done? she found herself wondering. How would it feel to love someone again that way? She loved Grace almost more than she could say, but the love she felt for her daughter was vastly different to the love shared by a man and a woman. Would it be possible to love Ross Tanner and let herself be loved by him in return?

The questions were too much for her to deal with. Heather turned away before Abby could notice there was anything wrong. She went straight to Resus and picked up the phone, although for a second she couldn't remember who she'd been intending to call. Her mind seemed to have locked onto the thought of how it would feel to fall in love again.

Warmth flowed through her as she recalled the simple pleasure of waking each morning to see Stewart lying beside her, of going home at the end of the day, knowing that he would be there to share all her triumphs and problems. They'd been so close that she'd felt she could tell him anything. Love like that was so rare that it seemed unlikely she would experience it again, unlikely but not impossible…

She stabbed in the numbers for the cardiac unit. She'd had her share of love and it had been wonderful while it had lasted and dreadful when it had ended. She wasn't going to put herself through that kind of torment again.

Ross handed over to the officer in charge of Blue Watch at the end of his shift. Although the blaze had been extinguished there was always a chance with this type of fire that it might re-ignite. Blue Watch would leave a crew on standby at the dock in case that happened.

Plans were also being formulated to bring in a team of experts to examine the remaining tanks and see if there was any oil beneath them before they were dismantled. It should have been done as a matter of course but Ross suspected it had been another cost-cutting exercise. Bradburn had probably decided it was unnecessary to pay for a professional survey when he could get one of his own men to do it free. Ross knew there would be an investigation into the cause of the fire but that would be very little consolation to the families of the men who had been killed and injured.

As he left the fire station he found himself thinking about the young man who had been so badly burned. Would Andy survive such terrible injuries? He followed the thought to its natural conclusion and sighed as he found himself wondering how Heather would react if the young man died. He couldn't stop himself worrying about her, especially when they had parted on less than friendly terms.

Whether it was worry for Heather or concern for the young man, Ross found himself heading toward St Gertrude's once he left work. It was only a short drive to the hospital so he found a parking space and bought a ticket from the pre-pay machine. He checked his watch as he strode across the car park, debating whether he should go directly to A and E to see Heather or if it would be better to find out how Andy was first. If the young man hadn't survived then he didn't want to put his foot in it and upset her further.

The receptionist informed him that Andy was in the burns unit after Ross had explained that he was one of the firemen who had attended the blaze at the docks. He took the lift to the fifth floor and followed the signs. There was nobody about so he knocked on the office door.

'I wonder if you could tell me how the young man who was brought in from that dockside fire is doing?' he asked the nurse who opened the door. 'His first name is Andy but I'm afraid I don't know his surname.'

'You aren't a relative?' She sighed when Ross shook his

head. 'I'm sorry but it's hospital policy not to give out information about a patient to anyone except a relative.'

'It's all right, Mary. I...I'll deal with this.'

Ross spun round when he recognised Heather's voice. He felt his heart skip a beat when he realised that she'd been crying. Without stopping to think, he went over to her and took hold of her hands.

'What's happened, Heather?' he demanded, although he suspected that he already knew the answer.

'Andy didn't make it. H-he died an hour ago.'

'I am so sorry, Heather.' He drew her into his arms and held her tightly, wishing there was something he could say to comfort her.

'He was only twenty and he had his whole life ahead of him. It's such a waste, such an awful, horrible *waste!*'

She drew back to look at him and Ross felt his heart leap when he saw the anguish in her eyes. In that moment, he knew that it wasn't just the death of a patient which had caused her such pain. This had something to do with what had happened in her past, but before he could ask her to explain, tears began to stream down her face.

'Why do dreadful things like this have to happen, Ross? Why?'

CHAPTER SIX

'IT'S coffee. I thought it might make a change from the usual tea.'

Heather jumped when Ross placed a steaming cup of coffee in front of her. They were in the foyer coffee-shop, although she hadn't the faintest idea how they'd got there. She didn't remember getting into the lift and travelling down to the ground floor. Everything was a blur apart from the fact that she remembered very clearly Ross holding her in his arms while she had cried her heart out.

The memory brought a rush of colour to her cheeks and she quickly picked up the cup. How could she have allowed herself to go to pieces like that? How could she have done so in front of Ross of all people? Granted, Andy's death had unleashed a flood of bitter memories but she should have tried harder to pull herself together. And yet in her heart she knew that nobody could have consoled her the way Ross had done.

The feel of his strong arms cradling her while she'd cried had made her feel safer than she'd felt in ages, and when he had started stroking her hair her anger had miraculously begun to fade. There wasn't a doubt in her mind that nobody but Ross could have provided the comfort she'd needed, and the realisation scared her. She couldn't allow herself to become dependent on him in any way.

'So how do you feel now?' Ross pulled out a chair and sat down. Heather could feel him watching her and her nervousness increased tenfold. What would he think if he discovered it had been the first time she'd cried in over three years?

'Heather?'

He prompted her to answer and she drove the thought from

her mind because it wouldn't help to dwell on it. 'I'm fine. Thank you.'

She took a gulp of the coffee to forestall any more questions and choked when she discovered how hot it was. She managed to swallow the hot liquid but it had already scalded her tongue. Tears started to her eyes again and she dashed them away. She'd managed to maintain her usual air of professional calm while the consultant in charge of the burns unit had been discussing Andy's case with her, but the moment she'd seen Ross she'd gone to pieces. It was as though he was able to touch her in a way that nobody had done for years.

'You're not fine, Heather. You're upset.'

He took the cup from her and blew gently on the hot liquid to cool it. It was such an unselfconsciously caring gesture that Heather was filled with a sense of wonder. How many men would think of doing such a thing? Yet when Ross did it, it seemed as natural as breathing.

He took a sip from the cup then put it on the table in front of her. 'Try that. It should be OK now.'

'Thank you.' She drank some of the coffee and summoned a smile when she saw him anxiously watching her. 'It's fine.'

'Good.' He grinned. 'I got plenty of practice checking the temperature of drinks when the twins were tiny. Any time Kate and Mike wanted to escape for an evening out, Uncle Ross was summoned to do his duty and babysit.'

'I'm surprised you didn't spatter a few drops of coffee on the inside of your wrist,' she said dryly, striving to match his tone. 'That is the approved method of testing the temperature of a baby's bottle.'

'So I believe. However, seeing as my sister breastfed the twins, I was never introduced to the delights of making bottles of formula. Kate used to feed the boys before she went out and always made sure she was back in time for the next round. So if it's water or juice then I'm a dab hand, but anything more complicated and I'll have to pass.'

'Well, the coffee's fine, you'll be pleased to hear,' she said lightly, trying not to dwell on the thought of Ross looking after

the twins when they'd been babies. It made her feel very
strange to imagine his large hands cradling their tiny bodies.
Maybe it was the fact that she had no experience of seeing a
man care for a baby that made it such an emotive idea, but
once again she found her eyes filling with tears.

'I know it's difficult, Heather, but you must have known
from the outset the odds were stacked against Andy.' Ross's
voice was filled with compassion.

'Yes, of course. I suppose I was hoping for some sort of a
miracle,' she murmured, relieved that he hadn't guessed the
real reason why she was crying.

'Sadly, miracles are few and far between.' Ross sighed regretfully. 'I hoped Andy would make it, too. I knew how upset
you'd be after all your efforts this morning.'

'You helped as well,' she pointed out, trying to stick to the
topic under discussion, although it wasn't easy. She had tried
not to dwell on the things she'd missed after Stewart had died,
but it was hard not to think about the role he would have played
in Grace's life. Heather could imagine his delight at being able
to bath and dress Grace, how gentle he would have been with
his precious daughter. Stewart would have treated Grace every
bit as tenderly as Ross had treated his nephews.

She frowned because it surprised her that she should have
compared the two men. Why had she felt the need to measure
Stewart against someone else when she'd always considered
him to stand head and shoulders above any other man?

She hurried on, uncomfortable with how disloyal it made her
feel. 'I would have had an even harder job setting up that line
if you hadn't been there to help me.'

'I was glad to help.' Ross reached across the table and
squeezed her hand. 'I mean that, Heather. I know you thought
I was annoyed about the amount of time I'd spent assisting you
this morning but you were wrong.' A rim of colour ran along
his cheekbones but he met her eyes without flinching. 'I apologise if I gave the impression that you were a nuisance. That
wasn't the case at all.'

Heather looked down at their joined hands, wondering what

it was about the way he'd said that which made her heart race. Ross had just been trying to clear up a misunderstanding and yet there'd been something about the tone of his voice that had added an extra dimension to the apology.

It was a relief when he released her and picked up his cup because Heather wasn't sure what she might have been tempted to say. Asking him what he had *really* meant was out of the question, but she was so out of touch with her own feelings that it was hard to understand other people's. And yet would it be wise to delve too deeply when she might not be able to deal with the problems it could unleash?

Her head spun as thoughts whirled inside it so that she missed what he said next. 'I'm sorry. What was that?'

'I was just wondering how the guy who was trapped in that warehouse had fared.'

'He's doing very well, I'm pleased to say. He's been taken to the coronary care unit with a suspected myocardial contusion...a bruised heart,' she explained when Ross raised his brows. She took a steadying breath and deliberately confined her thoughts to answering the question.

'The cardiac team is fairly confident there hasn't been too much damage done. A blow like that to the chest can severely damage the heart's valves and chambers. It can even rupture the aorta, although that hasn't happened in this instance. Obviously, the patient will need monitoring but so far, so good. The biggest problem, in fact, has been that he doesn't speak any English.'

'He's probably one of the illegal immigrant workers who were employed on the site. The site manager admitted that he had a number of men working for him who weren't listed on any official records. He said something about them being from Armenia.'

'I'll mention it to the cardiac team. They might be able to get someone in to translate for them.' She sighed. 'It probably explains why the poor fellow seemed so agitated. I had the devil of a job calming him down while I was examining him.'

'I expect he's worried about the authorities getting involved,'

Ross observed. 'Still, at least it seems as though he's going to make it. The number of fatalities could have been a lot higher, all things considered.'

'It could.' She finished her coffee and summoned a smile. 'I feel much better after that. Thank you.'

'My pleasure. Any time you need plying with tea—or coffee—and sympathy, you know who to call.'

It was said in the same light vein but Heather guessed it was just a cover. Ross wanted her to know he was there if she needed him but he didn't want to scare her. It surprised her how well he seemed to understand her. Normally, she took great care to keep some distance between herself and other people and it was alarming to know that Ross must have guessed that.

'That's very kind of you,' she said, hoping that he couldn't tell how on edge she felt. 'However, I don't normally go to pieces like that.'

'I'm sure you don't. Keeping control of your emotions is something you appear to be extremely good at, Heather. Maybe you've had a lot of practice at it?'

She knew he was probing for information but also knew it would be a mistake to tell him too much. Ross had been both kind and considerate and she appreciated everything he'd done for her, but she had to remember who and what he was. A searing pain lanced her heart but she couldn't afford to let it affect her judgement.

No matter how painful it was going to be, she had to bring their budding relationship to an end.

Ross could sense Heather withdrawing and bit back a sigh. It was a case of one step forward and two back where she was concerned. Every time he thought he'd gained a little ground he found it slipping away again. Why *was* she so reluctant to let him into her life? She didn't seem to have a problem in any physical sense. She certainly hadn't pulled away when he'd kissed her that morning, neither had she made any attempt to do so that evening when he'd been comforting her. Physically she wasn't repulsed by him but mentally she rejected him. It made him all the more determined to get to the bottom of what had happened in her past.

'I'm not someone who goes around making a song and dance about things, if that's what you mean.' She fixed him with one of her cool little smiles. 'It isn't in my nature.'

'Obviously, you're a paid-up member of the stiff-upper-lip brigade.'

He kept his tone light mainly because he didn't want to make an issue out of it. He also didn't want to make a fool of himself if by any chance he was wrong about some tragedy having shaped her life, although recalling what she'd told him about her fiancé dying maybe he already had his answer. Perhaps Heather preferred to keep her distance because she was still grieving for the man she'd loved?

The thought was so painful that Ross's hands clenched. He couldn't bear to think that Heather was still in love with the guy after all this time, and yet what could *he* do about it? What right did he have to try? Surely he should respect her feelings?

It was hard to deal with the sheer number of questions that rattled around inside his head so Ross didn't try. Maybe he was guilty of burying his head in the sand but he needed to find out more before he decided what to do. He finished his coffee then looked at Heather.

'If you've finished, I'll drive you home.'

'There's no need,' she said quickly. 'I'm perfectly fine now so I can catch the tube as I always do. Anyway, I'm not ready to leave just yet. I need to check that everything is all right in A and E before I can go home.'

'That's OK. There's no rush.'

Ross leant back in his chair and folded his arms. It was obvious that Heather didn't want him driving her home but there was no way he was prepared to let her make the journey by tube after the stressful day she'd had. He wouldn't have a moment's peace unless he knew she'd got home safely.

'I've nothing planned, apart from a date with a microwave

dinner. You certainly won't be ruining my evening if that's what's worrying you.'

He could tell that she was searching for another excuse to turn him down and settled back to hear what she would come up with this time. He glanced around the coffee-shop and realised that the place had started to fill up. Evening visiting would be starting shortly and there were a number of people having a break before they went to see their friends and relatives. There were even some members of staff seated at a table by the door. Ross saw one of the women glance at them then whisper something to her companions.

Heather must have noticed the group turning to look at them because Ross saw a tide of colour run up her face. It was clear how uncomfortable she felt about them attracting so much attention. She quickly pushed back her chair, obviously deciding that accepting his offer might be the lesser of two evils. 'I won't be long.'

'Take all the time you need. I'll wait here for you.' Ross treated her to a smile, although he couldn't help wondering if he'd been right to force her hand as he watched her leaving the coffee-shop. Perhaps he should have accepted her refusal rather than put her in such an awkward position.

He sighed. He was used to making on-the-spot decisions in his job and never doubting they were the right ones, too, but recently he'd found himself examining everything he did. Life had been so simple before he'd met Heather but he didn't regret it. It was as though he'd been only half-alive before she had appeared on the scene. It would be wonderful to think that one day Heather might come to feel the same way he did, but there was no point deluding himself. If her heart still belonged to another man then there was nothing left for him.

A and E was quiet when Heather arrived. It was almost seven and most of the day shift had gone home. There was just Ben left and he was in the treatment room, dealing with a child who had fallen off his bike. Heather went to see if she could help, although she knew the young registrar was perfectly capable of handling the case on his own.

She sighed as she knocked on the door and went into the room. Helping Ben was just a delaying tactic because she wanted to put off the moment when Ross would drive her home. Once they reached her flat she would have to make it clear that she didn't want to see him again. It wasn't going to be easy to make him accept her decision but she had no choice. She was far too vulnerable where Ross was concerned.

'I thought you'd gone home,' Ben remarked lightly when she appeared, but Heather could see the question in his eyes. She hurried to explain, not wanting him to think that she was checking up on him.

'I went to see a patient in the burns unit and it took longer than I'd expected. I thought I'd better make sure everything was quiet here before I went home.'

'Oh, I see.' Ben turned to the boy lying on the bed and winked. 'This is Dr Cooper, Tyson. She's the boss so you'd better be on your best behaviour.'

'Cool!' The boy grinned as he held up his hand. 'Nice to meet you, Boss-lady.'

'You, too, Tyson.' Heather laughed as she smacked the child's hand in a high-five greeting. 'So what have you been up to?'

'Fell off my bike while I was doing this *cool* jump. You should have seen how high I went.' The boy's face split into a huge smile. 'Best jump I've ever made, Doc. It was truly *awesome!*'

'Tyson is into bike scrambling in a big way,' Ben explained, gently examining the gash on the boy's forehead. 'His mum is waiting outside because she gets a bit queasy at the sight of blood, but she told me that he's training for the south-east junior championship.'

'You must be really good if you've reached that stage. Do you wear all the proper safety equipment?' Heather asked, moving closer as Ben took out a penlight and checked the boy's eyes. Both pupils reacted evenly to the light, a reassuring sign that the boy hadn't suffered a serious head injury.

'Course!' Tyson sounded disgusted. He didn't realise the reason why she'd asked him that question was to help to assess the level of injury he might have suffered. 'I wear the lot—helmet, knee and elbow pads, back protector. You have to wear the right clothes if you do a dangerous sport like scrambling. It's only dummies who take risks!'

'Of course. Sorry,' Heather apologised gravely. She smiled when Ben winked at her, although she couldn't help thinking how sensible the child was to take proper precautions. If only it were possible to safeguard against all life's dangers, she thought wistfully.

She hurriedly dismissed the thought when Ben turned to her. She agreed with him that all the boy needed was a couple of stitches to hold the cut together while it healed. She left Ben to deal with them and went to fetch her coat from the staff-room, but it was unsettling to admit that her mind had added a rider to that thought: *if only there was a way to protect Ross from the dangers of his job then there might not be a problem about them getting to know each other better.*

Heather closed her locker with hands that were no longer steady. Nobody could guarantee another person's safety, which was why it was imperative that she put a stop to what had been happening. After tonight, she wouldn't see Ross again.

It was almost seven-thirty by the time Heather reappeared. Ross had started to wonder if she might have skipped out on him when he saw her coming into the coffee-shop. Most of the visitors had left so he had a perfect view as she crossed the room.

His stomach muscles tightened as he watched the gentle sway of her hips as she came towards him. She was carrying her coat and all she had on was a tailored navy skirt and a white blouse. Her figure was trim but womanly, with full breasts and hips, a neat waist. The skirt flattened against her legs as she walked and Ross swallowed when he caught tantalising glimpses of her shapely thighs outlined beneath the fabric.

Heather was a truly beautiful and sensual woman yet she made no attempt to enhance her looks. Her clothes were neat but serviceable and he had never seen her wearing a scrap of make-up. It saddened him that she seemed determined not to take pleasure from her beauty. Maybe she *was* still grieving for the man she'd loved, but surely she understood that she had her own life to think about? If only he could make her understand that she had a future to look forward to and that *he* was more than willing to play a prominent part in it.

'Are you all right?'

Ross jumped when Heather touched him on the shoulder. He shot to his feet, almost overturning the chair in his haste. 'Fine. I was just wool-gathering. If you're ready, we may as well get off home.'

He summoned a smile but it was alarming to realise just how deep his feelings really were for this woman. He had never envisaged falling in love with someone who might not be able to love him in return, and he wasn't sure what to do about it. Surely it would be wiser to cut his losses and retreat with his dignity intact?

Ross squared his shoulders. Faint heart never won fair lady, or so the old adage claimed. He wasn't about to give up until Heather had made it clear there was no hope for him!

Heather could feel her nervousness increasing as Ross drove her home. She still hadn't worked out how to tell that she didn't want to see him again. She was tempted to tell him about Stewart but she simply didn't trust herself not to break down. The last thing she wanted was Ross showering her with sympathy when she needed to remain in control.

'Which way when we reach the crossroads?'

Heather jumped when Ross asked for directions. She could feel her heart pounding and had to make a conscious effort to calm down. 'Left. It's number 32A, halfway down on the right-hand side.'

'Fine.' Ross signalled and turned left. He drew up outside the house and switched off the engine. Rolling down the window, he studied the red-brick semi with obvious interest.

The house had been a single family dwelling until a few years ago when it had been divided into two flats. Heather had always considered herself extremely fortunate to have been in the estate agent's office when the ground-floor flat had come onto the market because finding suitable accommodation around London was a nightmare. Although the rent had been far more than she'd wanted to pay, the fact that access to the small back garden had come with the flat had persuaded her to stretch her budget. At least there was somewhere safe for Grace to play outside.

'This *is* nice,' Ross declared, turning to her. 'Have you lived here long?'

'Just over two years.' She took a quick breath because there was no point putting off telling him her decision any longer. 'Look, Ross—'

'Does your—?'

They both spoke together and both stopped. Ross chuckled but Heather could see a sudden wariness in his eyes. 'Ladies first.'

'No…please. What were you going to say?' Heather summoned a smile but the tension was making her nerves hum. How could she make him understand that she was right to end their involvement without hurting him? Suddenly, that seemed as important as making sure that *she* didn't get hurt.

'I was just going to ask if your mother lives with you or if she has a place of her own.'

'She lives here with me. It means that I don't have to worry about Grace if I'm delayed at work and there's no problem when I have to work nights either,' she explained as calmly as she could, although the way Ross was looking at her made her want to squirm in her seat. She couldn't remember when she'd seen such intensity in anyone's gaze before.

'It must be a big help, especially working the sort of hours you do.'

'It is. I don't know how I'd cope if Mum wasn't here. I hate the thought of having to put Grace into a nursery.'

'It also means that you have someone to babysit if you want to go out of a night, I imagine. I know one of my sister's biggest headaches is finding a reliable babysitter.'

'That isn't an issue,' she said quickly, because she had a horrible suspicion where the conversation was leading. She didn't want Ross to invite her out because it would make it that much more difficult to tell him that she couldn't see him again. 'I prefer to spend any free time I have with Grace. I see far too little of her as it is.'

'I understand that but you need a break from being a mother just as much as you need time out from your job.' He looked deep into her eyes. 'You should take some time for yourself, Heather.'

'I'm perfectly happy the way I am.'

'Are you? You can put your hand on your heart and swear that you don't want more out of life?'

'No! I've just explained that my life is fine the way it is,' she retorted. 'I'm sorry, Ross, but, frankly, I don't think it's any of your business how I choose to live.'

'Maybe it isn't but I still think you're missing out on an awful lot. Maybe you are happy with what you have, but surely you have other needs that neither your job nor your daughter can satisfy?'

Heather felt her face suffuse with heat when she realised what he meant. She'd never thought about her physical needs since Stewart had died but all of a sudden she couldn't stop the images that filled her head, images of Ross making love to her. She could picture him stripping off her clothes and carrying her to the bed, laying her down on it. She could imagine the passion on his face as he studied her naked body before his hands began to seek out all the secret places. The pictures were so vivid that she gasped when Ross touched her lightly on the knee.

'Heather, what is it?' he demanded urgently. 'What's wrong?'

'Nothing!'

She reached for the doorhandle, desperate to make her escape. All thoughts about how she would tell him that she couldn't see him again had fled. It wasn't the first time she'd felt sexual desire for Ross—she only wished it was. Maybe then it wouldn't feel like a complete betrayal of everything she'd felt for Stewart. Stewart had been the love of her life and losing him had been the worst thing that could have happened to her, yet she'd just sat there, imagining how it would feel if Ross made love to her!

'I'm sorry. That was completely out of order.'

There was a note of dejection in his voice that made her pause and she heard him sigh. 'I can't help how I feel, though, Heather. I care what happens to you.'

The frank admission brought a sudden mist of tears to her eyes but Heather blinked them away. She couldn't afford to dwell on how much it meant to hear him say that. She had to make it clear that there was no future for them and save them both getting hurt.

'But I don't want you to care about me, Ross. I know you mean well but the fact is that I'm not interested in having a relationship with you or anyone else.'

CHAPTER SEVEN

WELL, that had been perfectly clear!

'I see.' Ross summoned a smile but it was hard not to show how dismayed he was by Heather's announcement. 'I suppose I should thank you for being so direct.'

'It saves a lot of time, I always find.'

She got out of the car then glanced round when the front door of the house opened and a woman appeared. The woman was holding Grace and Ross saw the little girl bounce up and down in delight when she spotted Heather.

He got out of the car, not wanting to appear rude by driving away. The woman was obviously Heather's mother because he could see the resemblance as she came down the path. They were the same height and build, and had the same soft grey eyes and delicate features, he just had time to notice before Grace lurched towards him with her arms outstretched.

Ross automatically caught her. He laughed when the little girl chuckled. 'You're a little monkey. You knew I'd have to catch you, didn't you?'

'She's never done that before! She's normally so shy with strangers.'

Ross laughed at Mrs Cooper's astonishment. 'Ah, but I'm not a stranger, you see. Grace and I met the other day in the park and she must have remembered me. I'm Ross Tanner, by the way. And you must be Heather's mother.'

'Sandra Cooper.' Sandra informed him with a warm smile. She looked round as Heather joined them and Ross could see the question in her eyes. 'Grace seems to have taken to Mr Tanner in a big way. I can't remember her going to anyone like that before.'

'Maybe she's growing out of the clingy stage,' Heather said

tonelessly. She took the little girl from him, shaking her head when Grace tried to wriggle out of her grasp. 'No, that's enough, Grace. Ross has to go home now.'

Grace let out a loud yell of displeasure. 'Back! Back!'

'I seem to have started something.' Ross grimaced when he saw two fat tears roll down the child's cheeks. 'I don't mind holding her, honestly.'

'She has to learn that she can't have her own way all the time,' Heather said firmly. She gave the little girl a cuddle but Grace just cried all the harder.

'I expect she's tired,' Sandra explained apologetically. 'I kept her up so she could see you before she went to bed.'

'She's probably reached that stage where there's no reasoning with her.' Ross wiped the tears off the child's cheeks and smiled at her. 'That's a lot of noise for such a little girl. You're going to give your poor mummy a headache.'

'Back, back,' Grace repeated, trying to struggle out of Heather's arms so she could get to him.

Ross looked at Heather. He didn't want to appear as though he was questioning her judgement, but he hated to see the child getting so upset. 'I don't have to rush off right this very minute. It seems a shame to upset her when she's not really being naughty. I know what the twins can be like when they're tired.'

'Oh, so you have children, Mr Tanner?' Sandra put in quickly.

'Only on loan.' Ross laughed when he saw Sandra's bewilderment. 'My sister has twin five year-old boys. She's expecting another baby and has high blood pressure so I do my doting uncle bit as often as I can.'

'I see!' Sandra's face cleared. 'That explains why Grace is so comfortable with you. You're obviously used to being around children and she can sense that.'

Sandra turned to Heather. 'Why don't you let Mr Tanner hold Grace if it will calm her down, darling? It's tiredness rather than naughtiness, so I don't think it will hurt to let her have her own way for once.'

Heather sighed as she passed Grace to him. 'I suppose it won't matter just this once,' she conceded.

Ross settled the child in his arms, shaking his head in amusement when Grace immediately stopped crying and smiled at him. 'Happy now, are you?'

'Why don't we all go inside?' Sandra suggested. 'There's no point standing out here on the pavement.'

'I don't want to be a nuisance…' Ross began, unsure how Heather would feel about having him in her home.

'Of course you aren't being a nuisance!' Sandra declared, leading the way.

Ross glanced at Heather for guidance but she merely shrugged before she followed her mother into the flat. He followed more slowly, wondering if he was making a mistake by putting her in such an awkward position. He was under no illusions about her welcoming him into her home after the conversation they'd had, but she obviously didn't want to make a fuss in front of her mother.

He sighed. Talk about being stuck between a rock and a hard place!

Heather hung her coat in the hall then led the way to the sitting room. She knew that Ross had followed her but she didn't look round. She wanted to be sure that she had herself under control before she looked at him again.

'This is nice. Who does the decorating around here? You or your mother?'

Heather took a steadying breath before she turned, but even then she wasn't fully inured against the feelings that flowed through her when she saw Ross standing in the doorway with Grace in his arms. The little girl was snuggled against him, her head resting trustingly on his shoulder. They looked so *right* together but she knew it would be wrong to start thinking along those lines. Grace was Stewart's daughter and she had no connection whatsoever to Ross.

'I redecorated the flat before Mum moved in.' She glanced around the room, needing a few seconds to regain her composure. 'It took me ages to decide what colour to paint the walls. The previous tenants had painted the whole place white but I wanted to choose a colour that would warm everywhere up.'

'Well, you've certainly succeeded.' Ross cast an admiring glance at the rich terracotta walls and buttery-coloured woodwork. 'It looks really cosy in here. I wish my place looked half as good! Maybe I should get you to suggest a colour scheme. I'm hopeless at things like that.'

'I doubt I'd be much help,' she said quickly. 'It's difficult to make suggestions for colour schemes when you don't know a person very well.'

'There's an easy answer to that, Heather.'

Heather shivered when she heard the invitation in his voice. It was just too much, coming on top of what had happened already. She looked round in relief when her mother popped her head round the door.

'I've made a casserole, darling.' Sandra turned to Ross before Heather could reply. 'There's more than enough for two so you will stay for supper, Mr Tanner? I have to go out and you can keep Heather company. There's nothing worse than eating on your own.'

'I'm sure Ross is far too busy to keep me company,' Heather protested, shooting a speaking look at her mother.

'Nonsense! You heard Mr Tanner say that he didn't have to rush off.' Sandra checked her watch. 'I must go. I'm meeting David and I don't want to keep him waiting.'

Heather took a deep breath as the sound of the front door slamming announced Sandra's departure. Frankly, she wasn't sure what to do. Telling Ross that she didn't want him to stay would be so rude after he had taken the trouble to drive her home.

'Don't worry, I won't be staying. If you could just take Grace off me, I'll be on my way.'

Heather bit her lip when Ross settled a reluctant Grace in her arms. He'd obviously realised that she didn't want him to stay and it made her feel awful. After all, what harm could there be in them sharing a meal so long as she made it clear afterwards that she didn't intend to see him again?

'Please, stay,' she said quickly before she thought better of it. 'Consider it a small thank-you for driving me home.'

'I don't expect to be repaid for driving you home, Heather. I was more than happy to do so. And I most certainly don't want to impose on you,' he said bluntly.

'You're not.' A little colour touched her cheeks but she met his gaze steadily. 'I'm sorry if I appeared ungracious but Mum caught me off guard. I'd really like you to stay if you haven't anything planned. Why don't I see if I can get Grace settled in her cot and then we can eat? I don't know about you but I'm starving.'

'Thank you. I'd like to stay, then,' he said gravely. He glanced at Grace and chuckled. 'Although putting Grace down for the night sounds like wishful thinking to me. I hate to mention it but she looks as though she's getting her second wind!'

Right on cue, Grace suddenly demanded to be put down. Heather sighed as she watched her daughter run straight to the toy box. 'She's overtired, I'm afraid. It's going to take a while to settle her down.'

'Why don't I play with her while you fix supper?'

'Are you sure you don't mind?' Heather said hesitantly, wondering if it was fair to expect him to look after Grace after the busy day he'd had.

'Of course I don't mind.' Ross placed his hands on her shoulders and propelled her towards the door. 'Off you go. Grace will be fine with me.'

'OK. Thanks.' She smiled up at him, feeling her heart knock against her ribs when he smiled back. She hurried from the room and went straight to the kitchen, trying not to think about the expression she'd seen in his eyes, but it was impossible to shut it out.

A shiver ran through her. Ross had admitted that he cared about her and she could tell it was true. Whilst she couldn't help feeling elated by the thought, it also scared her. She simply couldn't afford to be swayed by his feelings, or her own for that matter. She had to stick to her decision and end their relationship because it was the right thing to do. She sighed. That didn't mean it was going to be easy to carry it through, though.

It didn't take long to heat up the casserole and put together a simple salad to go with it. Heather laid the kitchen table then went back to the sitting room to tell Ross the meal was ready. She paused in the doorway, drinking in the sight that met her.

Ross was sprawled out on the floor with a laughing Grace perched on his chest. The little girl was bouncing up and down, giggling like mad when he huffed and puffed each time she bounced on him. His dark hair was all mussed and the front of his white shirt was creased to rags, but he was obviously having as much fun as Grace was.

Heather felt warmth invade her as she watched them playing together. It was obvious they had formed a close bond in a remarkably short time, although it didn't really surprise her. Ross seemed to have a natural affinity with children and Grace responded to it. It made Heather wonder if she was doing the right thing by turning her back on what Ross could offer her and Grace. How wonderful it would be if her precious daughter had a father at last.

The thought shocked Heather so much that she gasped, and Ross must have heard her. He looked round and grinned when he saw her standing in the doorway. 'We're playing horsies and I'm the horse!'

'Rather you than me.' Heather summoned a smile but her heart was racing out of control. Grace's father was dead and nobody could ever replace him, so where had that idea sprung from?

'Hmm, sounds as though you've had more than your fair share of being Dobbin.' Ross lifted Grace off his chest and held her at arm's length. 'Right, then, young lady, the poor old horsy is tired out and wants his supper. We can play again another time.'

'More horsy, more horsy!' Grace demanded, kicking her feet

wildly. She caught Ross a glancing blow under his chin and he groaned.

'Whoa, steady on! If you knock out the poor old horse then you won't get another ride.'

'Are you all right?' Heather said anxiously, hurrying across the room and taking Grace from him.

'I'll live.' He wiggled his jaw from side to side then grinned at her. 'Although, if I were you, I'd think seriously about getting her some kick-boxing lessons when she's older. She's obviously a natural!'

Heather smiled. 'She used to kick up a storm when I was pregnant. I was convinced she was going to be a boy, in fact.'

'But instead she's a beautiful little girl who looks just like her mother,' Ross said deeply as he scrambled to his feet.

'I...I've always thought she looks more like Stewart than me,' Heather said huskily, because the way Ross was looking at her made it almost impossible to breathe properly.

'Because she doesn't have your colour hair and eyes?' Ross looked at Grace for a moment. His gaze returned to Heather and she felt her skin prickle when he subjected her to an intent scrutiny. 'Even so, she still looks very like you, Heather.'

'Does she?' She cleared her throat but she could hear the quaver in her voice and knew that Ross could hear it, too.

'Mmm. This little girl is going to be a real heartbreaker when she grows up—just like her mum.'

Heather wasn't sure what she should say to that. Anything she could think of seemed fraught with danger. She didn't want to break anyone's heart and especially not Ross's. It was a relief when he suddenly changed the subject.

'I take it that supper is ready?'

'Oh, um, yes,' she said hurriedly. She settled Grace on her hip and turned to lead the way. 'I hope you don't mind eating in the kitchen. We converted the dining-room into another bedroom when Mum moved in.'

'Of course I don't mind. I normally eat my meals off a tray in front of the television so actually sitting down at a table is really going upmarket for me!'

Heather laughed, feeling some of her tension ease a little. 'I'd probably do that, too, only I don't want Grace to get into bad habits.'

'Quite right, too. I expect I'll feel the same if and when I ever have any children of my own.'

'I'm sure you will,' she agreed, trying not to think about the family Ross would have one day. It made her feel very odd to imagine him and some unknown woman raising their children together.

She quickly strapped Grace into her high chair and gave her some building blocks to play with while she served their meal. She took the casserole out of the oven and spooned it onto the plates she'd had warming. She wasn't *jealous* at the thought of Ross showering affection on someone else—of course she wasn't! And yet she couldn't dismiss the feelings of envy at the thought of what a wonderful husband and father Ross would be.

'This is good. It's ages since I had a home-cooked meal.' Ross forked up another mouthful of chicken and sighed appreciatively. 'Take-aways and frozen dinners can't hold a candle to food like this.'

'Mum is a great cook. I'm really spoiled because she tends to do all the cooking when I'm at work.' Heather took some salad from the bowl then passed it to Ross.

'Thanks. I used to enjoy cooking when I was younger but I don't have the time now or the inclination.' He put the salad servers back in the bowl. 'It seems too much of an effort when you get in from work, doesn't it?'

'It does, although I used to enjoy cooking when Stewart and I had our first flat,' she said without thinking.

'I expect it's different when you're cooking for someone you love,' he observed quietly.

'I suppose it is.'

Heather applied herself to the meal, wishing that she hadn't mentioned Stewart's name. It made her feel uncomfortable to talk about him to Ross after all the strange thoughts that had invaded her head that evening. The sooner she took steps to get her life back on track the better it would be. She didn't need this kind of turmoil. She had to think about the effect it could have on Grace.

Ross must have sensed her reluctance to say anything else because he changed the subject. He kept up an undemanding conversation about the weather and current affairs while they finished their meal, and Heather was grateful to him. Grace was obviously getting tired because Heather could see her eyelids drooping when she got up to plug in the kettle.

'I'll make some coffee then put Grace to bed.'

'Why don't I make it while you see to Grace?' Ross suggested, standing up. He grinned at her. 'I should warn you, though, that my coffee is an acquired taste.'

'That sounds ominous.' Heather rolled her eyes. 'In that case, shall we have instant? There's less likelihood of anything going wrong.'

'Don't bet on it,' he replied cheerfully. 'Do you like your coffee strong or weak, by the way?'

'I'll leave it to you. Coffee's in that jar and milk is in the fridge. If you take sugar then there's some in the cupboard over the stove.' She unstrapped Grace's safety harness and lifted her out of the high chair. 'We'll leave you to it, then. Say night-night to Ross, darling.'

'Night-night,' Grace repeated sleepily, snuggling against her mother.

'Sweet dreams, poppet.'

Ross bent and dropped a gentle kiss on the child's head. Heather's pulse leapt when she felt his hair tickling her cheek. She turned away and hurried from the room because the urge to linger was just too strong.

There was no future for them, she told herself sternly as she laid Grace down in her cot. She knew that and she must make sure that Ross understood it, too. However, she couldn't deny that her heart was aching at the thought of having to tell him that she didn't want to see him again.

Ross had made the coffee when she went back to the kitchen.

Heather sat down and picked up her cup. She took a cautious sip of the hot liquid and raised her brows. 'It tastes fine to me.'

'Good, although it's probably a case of good luck rather than good judgement.' He drank some of his coffee then put the mug down carefully on the table. 'I've enjoyed tonight, Heather. Thank you for asking me to stay.'

'You're welcome,' she replied politely, feeling her heart quicken because the moment was fast approaching when she would have to tell him her decision.

'Maybe we could do it again some time. How would you feel about coming out for dinner with me one evening?'

'I don't think so. I'm sorry, Ross, but I think it's time we both faced facts.'

'Fact number one being that you aren't interested in going out with me?' He laughed but Heather could see the pain in his eyes and felt terrible. It took every bit of courage she possessed to carry on.

'There's no point. I have an extremely demanding job and what little free time I have I spend with Grace, as I told you. There simply isn't room in my life for…' She stumbled, unsure how to describe what Ross wanted from her.

'Friendship? You've made it clear that you aren't interested in a relationship and I accept that. However, that doesn't mean we can't be friends. It's your choice, Heather. I would never try to persuade you to do something you weren't happy with.'

His voice was so wonderfully warm and persuasive that Heather found herself weakening. Did she really need to end their involvement if Ross would be happy for them to remain strictly friends?

She stared at her cup while she thought it all through, but if they were facing facts then she had to face the fact that Ross wanted her as a man wanted a woman, not as a friend. She'd been aware of how he felt from the beginning, even though she had shied away from admitting it. And while she was being honest, she had to be truthful about her own feelings. She wanted him, too. Realistically, how could she expect them to remain simply as friends?

Heather's heart was aching when she looked up. Ross was sitting across the table from her and for a moment she allowed herself the pleasure of looking at him. He was everything a woman could want—kind, caring, brave and handsome—but that was what made him so dangerous.

'Ross, I...'

'It's OK. You don't have to say anything. I know when I'm beaten.'

He treated her to a wry smile but the sadness in his eyes was more than she could bear. Without pausing to think, she leant forward and kissed him on the cheek. He smelled of soap and fresh air all mingled with a scent that was purely his own. She inhaled deeply, knowing the memory would linger long after he'd gone, a poignant reminder of what might have been if things had been different.

'I'm sorry, Ross,' she whispered as she drew back.

'And I'm sorry, too, Heather. More sorry than I can tell you.' He touched her lightly on the cheek then stood up. 'Thanks again for the meal. Please, don't get up. I'll see myself out.'

Heather closed her eyes as he left the room. She knew it was silly but she couldn't bear to watch him leaving. It was only after she'd heard the front door closing that she opened her eyes, although for a moment she couldn't see because of the tears that blurred her vision.

Ross had gone and she wouldn't see him again. She'd stuck to her decision and she'd been right to do so. If only it didn't feel as though she'd made the biggest mistake of her life.

'Red Watch...fall out!'

Ross went straight to the office after roll call had finished. It was Wednesday evening and the crew of Red Watch were coming to the end of their turn on night duty. He had the next four days off and he wasn't looking forward to having so much free time on his hands. It was three weeks since he'd seen Heather and not a day had passed when he'd not thought about her.

He sighed as he took a file out of the cabinet and sat at his desk. The annual budget was due for review and he needed to complete his report so that it could be presented at the next council meeting. There had been talk of closing Rosedale fire station and he wanted to make it clear that Hexton would be unable to provide adequate cover if that happened. Nevertheless, despite how urgent the matter was, he found his mind returning to what had happened between him and Heather that last night. Why had she kissed him if she didn't care?

The shrill summons of the emergency telephone coming from the watch room was a welcome distraction from a question which he'd spent far too much time trying to answer. Ross left the office and hurried downstairs to see what was happening. Terry Green had the details by the time Ross arrived.

'Some lunatic has tried to climb the London Eye and got stuck halfway up,' Terry informed him.

'I thought they had security guards on duty to stop people doing damned fool things like that,' Ross exclaimed.

'Apparently it's one of the security staff who's decided to climb it,' Terry explained wryly, pressing the bell to summon the crew. 'They've stopped the Eye but now there are several hundred people stranded above London.'

'Oh, great! Just what we need. Let's hope that nobody panics.'

Ross headed for the fire engine, trying not to think about what they could have on their hands. He consoled himself with the thought that all the capsules attached to the giant wheel would remain securely locked. Nobody would be able to climb out but it still meant there must be a lot of anxious people up there.

'Make sure we've got enough ropes on board,' he directed. 'It sounds as though it's going to be a climbing job. I doubt if the ladder will be long enough to reach this guy if he's halfway up the Eye.'

'At least everyone who bought a ticket tonight will get their money's worth,' Jack put in, climbing into the cab and starting the engine. 'Not only will they get an extended bird's-eye view of London but there's a rescue being thrown in for good measure.'

'I wonder if we'll make the evening news?' Baz Russell, the newest member of the team, glanced out of the window as the fire engine pulled out of the station. 'Shame it's raining. The camera crews mightn't be too keen to hang around on such a rotten night. My mum would be thrilled to bits if she saw me on the ten o'clock news.'

Ross didn't say anything as the others added their own comments. There was always a lot of chatter on the way to a shout. It was a way of letting off steam. The crew were well aware how difficult and dangerous it was going to be to get the man down in conditions like these, yet every one of them was prepared to put his own life on the line to help.

Ross was proud to be a member of the brigade. He loved the job even if it was extremely dangerous at times. He frowned. Did his job have any bearing on Heather's decision not to get involved with him? Maybe he was clutching at straws, but he couldn't dismiss the idea.

'Suspected carbon monoxide poisoning. ETA five minutes. Where's Ben? He should have been back from his break by now.'

'I'll take it.' Heather shook her head when Abby frowned. 'I don't mind. It's been like a madhouse in here tonight. Ben deserves a few extra minutes.'

'Maybe he does, but you'll wear yourself out if you keep on like this, Heather.' Abby put her hands on her ample hips. 'Just because you're senior reg in the unit, it doesn't mean that you have to do double the work of everyone else.'

'I don't!'

Heather laughed off the accusation, although she knew the sister had made a valid point. In the past three weeks she'd been shouldering far more of the workload than she should have done. Granted, the continued lack of a consultant meant that she'd had to pick up a lot of tasks that normally she wouldn't have had to tackle, but most of the extra work she'd done had been from choice. It was just easier if she kept herself busy because it gave her less time to brood.

She shut off that thought because she didn't want to start thinking about Ross again. So maybe she *did* miss him but she'd done what she had to do. Anyway, he'd probably found someone else by now and forgotten all about her.

'Any information about where the patient was found and how long he or she had been breathing in the gas?' she asked crisply, refusing to dwell on how much that idea hurt.

'It's a she and she was found in the bathroom,' Abby explained, following Heather into Resus. 'No idea how long she'd been in there, though.'

'We're going to need her blood gases done as quickly as possible so get onto the lab and warn them, will you?' Heather snapped on a pair of gloves when she heard the sound of a siren approaching. 'We'll need to know what degree of carbon monoxide saturation she's suffering.'

'Will do!' Abby hurried to the phone as the doors opened and the paramedics wheeled in the patient.

'Alison Clark, nineteen, a student,' Frank Farnell rattled out. 'She was found unconscious in the bathroom. Pulse 120, respiration 25. We've administered oxygen but she hasn't regained consciousness.'

'Thanks, Frank. Let's get her onto the bed. On my count—one, two, three.' Heather bent over the girl as the paramedics left and began to examine her. Alison was unconscious and her face was flushed a deep cherry-red colour.

'I thought our tutor was exaggerating when he told us about the colour of a person's face when they've suffered carbon monoxide poisoning,' Rob Bryce exclaimed as he hurried into Resus.

'It is very striking,' Heather agreed. 'It's due to the amount of carboxyhaemoglobin in the blood. The carbon monoxide binds with the haemoglobin and prevents it carrying oxygen around the body. Because carbon monoxide is odourless, most people don't realise they are being poisoned until it's too late.'

'Her friend came in the ambulance with her. She told me there's an old gas water heater in the bathroom of their flat and that they've complained to the landlord because it hasn't been working properly,' Rob told her. 'He kept promising to get someone to look at it but nobody ever came.'

'If he failed to have the appliance serviced on a regular basis then the police could decide to prosecute him.' Heather glanced at the young student and sighed. 'Not that it will be much comfort to her family if she doesn't pull through.'

Abby took blood and sent it to the haematology lab. Heather finished her examination and delegated one of the junior nurses to sit with the girl while they waited for the results to come back. Alison was receiving one hundred per cent oxygen but there was no sign of her regaining consciousness, which was extremely worrying. Carbon monoxide acted on the brain and if enough of the gas was inhaled, it caused irreversible changes to the central nervous system.

There was little else she could do for the girl so, mindful of Abby's nagging, Heather went to the canteen for her break. She wasn't really hungry but she had a cup of tea and a sandwich then went back to the unit. The lab results had come back and they showed that Alison's carbon monoxide saturation reading was almost fifty per cent, which was dangerously high.

Heather phoned the bed manager and asked him to find a high-dependency bed for the girl then had a word with her friend and advised her that Alison's parents should be told about what had happened. Although Heather didn't say so, she knew it would be touch and go whether or not Alison survived.

It was after midnight by the time she'd got everything sorted out and the department was starting to quieten down. Heather decided that she'd better write up some notes and headed for the office, but just as she opened the door, Ben called her.

'We've got a woman on her way in. She collapsed at home and one of her children phoned for an ambulance. She's pregnant but the paramedics aren't sure how far along she is because she's unconscious.'

'We'd better inform Maternity. Sounds like it could be one for them.' Heather groaned as she closed the office door. 'And here was I thinking I could get on with some paperwork. I should have known better.'

'You should,' Ben agreed. 'Still, keeping busy will help to take your mind off whatever it is that's been bothering you lately.'

'What do you mean?' Heather asked in astonishment.

'It's obvious you've been worrying about something, Heather. I'm not trying to pry but if you ever need a friendly ear then mine is available.'

'Thanks,' she murmured as Ben turned to speak to a patient who was leaving.

She went to the door to wait for the ambulance but she couldn't pretend that the young registrar's comment hadn't worried her. She'd believed that she'd been hiding her feelings as she always did, but apparently not. It just seemed to prove how deeply Ross had affected her. He had slid past her defences, found a niche in her life, and she couldn't pretend that she didn't miss him. She'd been right to send him away, though. If he'd had this much of an effect after such a short time then how much worse would it have been if she'd let their involvement continue?

There was little comfort to be gained from that thought, however, so Heather was glad when the ambulance arrived and she could turn her attention to other matters. She waited while the crew opened the rear doors, expecting them to immediately lift out the patient. What she hadn't expected to see were the two small boys clutching the paramedic's hands. She gasped in dismay. What on earth were Ross's nephews doing here?

It was almost one a.m. by the time Red Watch got back to the station. Rescuing the man from the London Eye had been an experience Ross hoped he would never have to repeat. The ladder hadn't been long enough to reach the man so it had been a hands-on climbing job.

The fact that the rain had continued throughout the evening had increased their problems. Baz and Jack had done a fantastic job by bringing the man safely down. A number of people who'd been stranded in the capsules had been deeply shocked by the experience but there had been no actual casualties. It had been a successful operation but Ross was as relieved as the men were when they pulled into the station.

'That was a job well done,' he said to the crew. 'Let's hope the police read that guy the Riot Act and stop him doing anything as stupid again.'

'He told me his girlfriend had dumped him,' Baz informed them as they climbed down from the fire engine. 'Most blokes in his position would just go off and drown their sorrows, but obviously that wasn't dramatic enough for him!'

Ross left the men discussing the night's events and hurried upstairs. He needed a change of clothes first then he would have to get on with his report. He'd just reached the landing when he heard the office phone ringing, and he veered off to answer it.

'Tanner.' Clamping the receiver between his ear and his left shoulder, he started to peel off his soaking wet T-shirt. The rain hadn't abated all night and he'd had to strip off his waterproof clothing while he'd climbed part of the way up the Eye with the men.

'Ross, it's Heather.'

Ross just caught the receiver before it hit the desk. He dragged the T-shirt over his head and tossed it onto the floor, aware that his hands were shaking. 'This is a surprise. I didn't expect to hear from you again,' he said in a massive understatement.

'No, I'm sure you didn't.' There was a small pause before she hurried on. 'Look, I'm sorry to drop this on you without any warning, but your sister has been brought in to A and E.'

'Kate! But what's the matter with her? Is it the baby?' he demanded, his stomach plummeting with shock.

'We think she must have tripped and fallen down the stairs. The boys have no real idea what had happened because they just heard her cry out. Fortunately, they knew how to phone for an ambulance. I've examined her and it's obvious that she has a nasty bump on her head. The baby seemed to be in distress so Kate has been sent to Theatre for an emergency Caesarean.'

'But she's going to be all right?' His hand clenched on the receiver when she didn't answer immediately. 'Heather?'

'We can't be sure yet, Ross. That's the honest answer. She's unconscious and her Glasgow coma score is very low. Once the baby has been delivered, Kate will be sent for a CT scan. We should have a better idea then how much damage she did when she hit her head.'

'I'll be there as soon as I can. Should I come straight to A and E?' he demanded, trying to make sense of what he'd heard. He gasped as a thought occurred to him. 'What about the twins? They're in the house on their own—'

'They're here,' she cut in quickly. 'In fact, they're in my office at the moment, playing with some toys. They're perfectly safe, Ross, but I'm sure they will be glad to see you because they were very frightened when they arrived.'

'Tell them I'll be there as soon as I can. And, Heather?'

'Yes?'

'Thank you.'

'You don't have to thank me, Ross. I want to help.' She paused then added quietly, 'That's what friends are for.'

Ross replaced the receiver and stared across the room. Had Heather meant that? Did she want them to be friends now, even though she'd sent him away?

He took a deep breath because this wasn't the time to start debating the issue. He phoned HQ, explained he had a family crisis and needed to leave the station then handed over to his second in command. Ten minutes later he was in his car.

He started the engine, uttering a heartfelt prayer that Kate would be all right. At least Heather had been there when Kate had been admitted, and that meant his sister had received the very best possible care. He would trust Heather with his life.

A wave of longing hit him. If only Heather would trust him, he knew he could make her happy.

CHAPTER EIGHT

'WILL we be able to see Mummy soon?'

'Not for a little while yet, I'm afraid.' Heather sat down and put her arms around the two boys. The twins were obviously upset about not being able to see their mother.

'Mummy's with some other doctors who are going to help her have the baby,' she explained gently. 'But I've spoken to Uncle Ross and he said to tell you that he'll be here soon.'

'Mummy won't die, will she?' Josh's lower lip started to wobble and Heather hugged him.

'Mummy is going to be fine,' she said firmly, mentally crossing her fingers that she wasn't being overly optimistic. However, the twins were far too young for her to explain the true nature of the situation to them. She gave Luke a hug as well then stood up.

'How about we go and find something for you to eat? I expect you're both hungry.'

The boys immediately followed her to the door. They were still wearing their pyjamas and Heather grinned as she took hold of their hands. 'It's a good job you have different coloured pyjamas or I wouldn't be able to tell you apart!'

'Lots of people can't,' Luke told her seriously. He was the more confident of the two brothers and tended to speak for both of them. 'They think I'm Josh and that Josh is me. Mummy can tell the difference, though, and Daddy can. Uncle Ross can as well, though sometimes we swap 'jamas when he's babysitting and fool him.'

'I imagine it's great fun, being able to do that,' Heather said, laughing. With their blond hair and huge brown eyes the twins were real little charmers. Despite the difference in their colouring, she could see a definite resemblance to Ross and her heart turned over when she found herself wondering what his children would look like if and when he ever had any.

'Uncle Ross calls us little monsters when we play tricks on him, but he doesn't really mind,' Josh said shyly. He stared wistfully up at her. 'Will he be here soon?'

'Just as soon as he can,' Heather assured him.

She took the boys to the vending machine and let them choose what they wanted, hoping that Ross wouldn't mind them having chocolate bars and cans of cola at that hour of the morning. Once they had everything they wanted, she took them back to her office and got them settled with some paper and crayons that she'd found in Reception.

'Why don't you each draw a picture for your mummy?' she suggested. 'I'll just go and see if Uncle Ross has arrived.'

The boys nodded, their mouths too full of chocolate to speak. Heather quickly made her way to the nursing station and phoned Theatre first to check how Kate was faring. She sighed in relief when one of the staff informed her that the baby had been delivered safely and was on its way to the nursery.

'Heather.'

She swung round when she recognised Ross's voice, feeling her heart go into overdrive when she saw him standing behind her. There were beads of rain in his dark hair and lines of strain etched into his face, but after an absence of three weeks he looked good enough to eat!

'There's nothing wrong with the baby, is there?'

'Oh, no!' Heather rushed to reassure him when she realised he had interpreted her silence as bad news. 'Kate's had a little girl, six pounds two ounces in weight. She's absolutely fine. She's on her way to the nursery so you'll be able to see her there.'

'Thank heaven for that!'

Heather saw a deep shudder pass through him. It was obvious the effort he was making to keep control of himself, and her heart went out to him. She laid her hand on his arm, wanting to make the situation as easy as possible for him. She didn't want Ross getting hurt if there was anything she could do to help.

'Once they've finished with Kate in Theatre, she will be going down to Radiology,' she explained huskily, shocked by the depth of her feelings. She might have ended their involvement but she couldn't pretend that she didn't care about Ross.

'She hasn't regained consciousness?' he asked in concern.

'No.' Heather drew him aside so Melanie could use the phone. There had been a fight outside a local nightclub and there were a number of people waiting to be seen. Heather knew that she would have to lend a hand soon but she wanted to make sure that Ross understood the situation first.

She led him to the relatives' room, waiting until she had closed the door before continuing the conversation. 'Kate is still unconscious and we need to find out why. That's why she'll be having a CT scan.'

'Have you no idea at all?' he demanded, pacing the floor.

'As I told you earlier, she hit her head when she fell and that's the most obvious explanation.'

'But is it normal for someone to be unconscious this long if they've just had a bump on the head?' He stopped in front of her and Heather could see the worry in his eyes.

'No, it isn't.' She sighed because there was no way she could avoid giving him a truthful answer. 'It could turn out that there's some damage to the brain—maybe a blood clot that's formed or possibly localised swelling. Either of those can cause a prolonged loss of consciousness but we won't know for sure until we get the results of the scan.'

'I see.' Ross ran his hand over his face and Heather could see that he was trembling. He grimaced when he saw her watching him. 'Sorry. You'd think I'd be used to dealing with bad news but it's different when you're personally involved.'

'It is and there's no need to apologise. I…I know how it feels, believe me.'

It was impossible to keep the pain out of her voice and she saw Ross's gaze sharpen. She turned away because the last thing she needed was to have to think about what she'd been through when Stewart had died.

'I'll fetch the boys. I kept them in my office because it was easier to see what they were up to while I was working. They'll be glad to see you because they are really worried about their mother.'

'It's good of you to have gone to so much trouble, Heather.'

He smiled when she looked round but she saw the question in his eyes. She knew without having to ask that he was wondering if she'd meant what she had told him on the phone.

Had she? Could she envisage them being friends when a few weeks ago she hadn't believed it possible? But three weeks ago she hadn't realised how much she was going to miss him…

'It was nothing,' she said quickly, before she could say something she might regret. She deliberately hardened her heart when she saw the disappointment on his face but it would be wrong to mislead him when she needed to think about what she was doing. 'I'll get the boys for you.'

She hurried from the room, closing the door before she made herself take several calming breaths, but even then her heart was racing. If only she could give Ross what he wanted then it would be so much easier, but she was too afraid to let down her guard in case she ended up getting hurt.

The twins were busily drawing when Heather went to the office. She helped them gather up their paper and crayons and took them to see Ross. They ran straight to him and he picked them up and hugged them tightly.

'It's going to be all right,' he told them gruffly, kissing each tousled blond head in turn. 'The doctors and nurses will make Mummy better.'

'Will you help make Mummy better as well, Heather?' Josh asked, turning to look at her with trusting brown eyes.

'I'll try my best,' she promised with a lump in her throat. Just witnessing how much Ross loved the twins had touched her deeply. It reminded her of what she'd been thinking earlier, about him having children of his own. There was no doubt in her mind that he would make the most wonderful father. If only Grace had someone like Ross to love and cherish her, she thought wistfully.

'Thank you, Heather.'

Ross had carried the twins across the room and Heather jumped when she discovered that he was standing right in front of her. Her breath caught when he bent and kissed her on the cheek. He drew back and she felt heat envelop her when she saw the tenderness in his eyes.

'Thank you for everything you've done tonight. We mean that from the bottom of our hearts, don't we, boys? So say thank you to Heather.'

'I…um… You're welcome,' Heather murmured as the twins obediently added their thanks.

She hurriedly excused herself and went to Reception. Her next patient was a young man who'd been hit over the head with a bottle in the nightclub affray and had a nasty scalp wound. He was extremely drunk and seemed to think it highly amusing to curse as loudly as he could as she took him to a cubicle, but his foul language went straight over Heather's head. All she could hear was the warmth in Ross's voice when he had thanked her, and nothing could sully the memory, not even a stream of ugly curses. It had been the moment when she'd realised how easy it would be to fall in love with him if she carried on seeing him.

Her heart was heavy as she got the young man settled on the bed. She'd been right to send Ross away three weeks ago and it would be wrong to go back on that decision no matter how much she longed to do so. Another hero in her life would be one hero too many.

The twins had finally fallen asleep on the sofa. Ross had spent over an hour trying to reassure them that Kate would be fine. He covered them with a blanket one of the nurses had brought him then sighed as he looked at their exhausted little faces.

The poor kids were worn out by what had happened and their ordeal wasn't over yet. The doctors were assessing the results of Kate's CT scan and although he hoped and prayed the news would be favourable, he had to prepare himself for the worst. Josh and Luke were going to need him if anything happened to their mother.

Ross swung round, hating himself for thinking such a thing when it felt as though he was tempting fate. He went into the corridor, wondering if he could find someone to watch the boys while he phoned his brother-in-law. It was going to be a big shock for poor Mike and Ross wasn't looking forward to having to break the news to him.

The sound of voices made him glance round and he felt his heart lift when he saw Heather coming along the corridor. She was deep in conversation with a tall man with grey hair and seemed unaware that Ross was standing there so he allowed himself the simple pleasure of watching her. The night had obviously taken its toll on Heather, too, because he could see how tired she looked. However, neither the shadows under her eyes nor the frown lines on her forehead could detract from her beauty.

His gaze moved on, centred on her mouth, and he felt his pulse quicken because there was no doubt that Heather had the most beautiful mouth he'd ever seen. Her lips were both sensually full yet delicately shaped with that perfect Cupid's bow. Ross could tell that she wasn't wearing lipstick and knew that their warm pink colour owed itself to nature rather than cosmetics. He was suddenly overwhelmed by a need to see if her mouth tasted as good as he remembered it to be. He'd only kissed her that one time all those weeks ago and it was hard to believe her lips really had been so soft and sweet....

'This is Mr Martindale, Ross, Head of Neurosurgery. He'd like to speak to you about Kate's CT scan.'

Ross jumped like a startled cat. He couldn't believe that he'd allowed himself to get so carried away. 'Mr Martindale,' he said, hurriedly shaking the man's hand. 'What have you discovered?'

'Maybe we could go inside to talk,' the consultant suggested, glancing into the relatives' room. He sighed when he saw the two small boys fast asleep on the sofa. 'Ah. It seems a shame to wake them.'

'You can use my office,' Heather offered immediately. She turned to Ross and smiled, but he could see the worry in her eyes. His spirits plummeted because it was obvious that Heather knew it wasn't good news about Kate. 'I'll keep an eye on the twins for you. I'm due for a break now so it won't be a problem.'

'Thanks,' he murmured distractedly. He followed the consultant into the office, steeling himself for what was to come, but it was hard to control his fear about what the other man would tell him.

'There's no point beating about the bush, Mr Tanner. It will only waste time we really don't have.' James Martindale didn't bother sitting down. 'Your sister has a large haematoma—a blood clot—on the right side of her brain, and we need to remove it as soon as possible.'

'You're saying that Kate will need an operation?' Ross sank onto a chair as his legs gave way.

'Yes. It's vital that we remove the clot before any more pressure builds up inside Mrs Lawrence's skull. We want to minimise the risk of further damage.'

'You mean that she might already have suffered some sort of brain damage?' Ross swallowed but the thought of Kate being left permanently disabled was almost more than he could bear.

'I'm afraid I can't answer that question, Mr Tanner.' The consultant sighed. 'You have to understand that the brain is a highly complex and delicate instrument and it's impossible to foretell how much or how little damage might have occurred as the result of an injury. All I can say is that the sooner we remove the clot, the better your sister's chances will be. We shall need a consent form signed before the operation can go ahead. Normally Mr Lawrence would be asked to sign it but I believe he's abroad at the present time.'

'That's right. I was just about to phone Mike and tell him

what's happened. He's working in the Arab Emirates and I'm not sure how long it will take him to get home.'

'In that case, perhaps you would sign in his stead? It's quite in order for a relative to give permission for an operation to proceed when the next of kin is absent and time is of the essence.'

'Of course I'll sign it,' Ross agreed immediately. 'I'll do anything if it will help Kate. When do you plan to operate?'

'Immediately.' James Martindale shrugged. 'The operation itself is fairly routine. I've performed it many times and I'm not anticipating any problems today. I wish I could be as confident of the prognosis but until your sister regains consciousness then we won't know what kind of problems there might be.'

'I understand, but what could it mean for Kate? What sort of problems might she have to face in the future?' Ross demanded anxiously.

'Patients who have suffered a severe head injury can be left both physically and mentally disabled. However, it would be wrong to try to second-guess the outcome at this stage, Mr Tanner. My advice to you is to try and remain positive. Your sister may be one of the lucky ones and make a complete recovery.'

'Yes, of course. Thank you,' Ross murmured.

He got up after the consultant had left and went to the window. It was almost six a.m. and there were lights coming on in the tower blocks overlooking that part of the hospital. He could imagine the people in those flats going about their normal, everyday routines. Nothing felt normal to him, though. His sister could be left severely handicapped and there was nothing anyone could do about it. He'd never felt more helpless in his life.

'Ross?'

He turned when he heard Heather's voice, not even feeling surprised when he saw her. He'd known she would come to find him because she understood how he must feel. In a funny kind of way it helped to lessen his pain to know that he didn't need to explain how devastated he felt.

He opened his arms, praying she would find the courage to give him the support he desperately needed, and he wasn't disappointed. She hurried across the room and stepped into his embrace, laid her head on his shoulder and wrapped her arms around his waist as though holding him was the most important thing she'd ever done. Tears welled in his eyes at the thought and he buried his face in her hair.

'Thank you,' he whispered roughly.

'What for?'

Her breath clouded on his cheek as she tipped back her head to look at him, and a spasm of raw need shot through his body like a dart of lightning. Ross's arms tightened as he drew her closer, needing to feel her softness against him to ease the pain.

'For being brave enough to let me hold you like this.'

'Oh, Ross.' The words were choked off by a sob and he sighed when he realised that she was crying.

'Don't cry, sweetheart,' he murmured, brushing her forehead then her cheeks with his lips. 'I didn't mean to upset you.'

'I know you didn't. It's just…just…' She swallowed and Ross could tell that she was struggling for control. He wasn't sure what she was trying to say but it didn't really matter. What mattered was that Heather was upset now and he needed to comfort her as she had tried to comfort him.

His mouth slid down her cheek and came to rest at the corner of her mouth. He ached to kiss her properly but knew it would be wrong to assume that was the kind of comfort she needed. He could taste the saltiness of her tears and hated to think that he might never again enjoy the sweetness of her kiss. He was steeling himself to let her go when she suddenly turned….

Their mouths met, clung, then parted as though the kiss had been too much for both of them. Ross was swamped by a host of sensations all at once. Heather's lips had tasted so sweet that he wished he could bottle their flavour so that he could savour it again and again. They'd felt so wonderfully soft and smooth that it had been like kissing warm satin. Even the tiny sigh that had escaped her had been so delicious that he wanted to commit it to memory like a much-loved tune. Everything about the kiss had been perfect, but would a second be as good?

He bent towards her at the same moment as she rose on tiptoe and their mouths met with a small jolt that rippled through his body. Ross could feel every cell tingling from the aftershocks and groaned in delight.

His arms tightened around her, kept her poised on tiptoe while his mouth plundered hers. He was just as aware of the softness and sweetness of Heather's lips this time but this kiss was very different to the first. There was so much emotion in it, so much need and raw longing, that it made his head reel. There wasn't a doubt in his mind that Heather wanted this kiss every bit as much as he did and the thought tipped him over the edge.

He nipped gently at her lower lip, tempting it to open so that he could explore the inner sweetness of her mouth. He could have shouted for joy when her lips parted if he hadn't been too busy taking full advantage. His tongue darted inside her mouth, found hers and then retreated because the sensations rushing through him were too much to deal with.

Had he ever felt this depth of desire before, this need to take everything Heather could give him and give her even more back in return? he wondered in amazement. He wanted her so much both physically and spiritually that he was actually shaking. In that moment Ross realised that the kind of happiness he'd always dreamed about was within his grasp, but it all depended on how Heather felt.

Did she—*could she*—feel for him even a fraction of what he felt for her?

Heather could feel her resistance melting like morning mist beneath the heat of the sun. Every single rule she had lived by during the past three years suddenly made not a scrap of sense. She wanted Ross to kiss her and hold and eventually…no, sooner than that…make love to her, so why pretend? Why not tell him how she felt?

She opened her mouth to do just that when there was a knock on the door. Heather automatically looked round, although for a second she had difficulty remembering where she was. Her mind was too full of the delights of Ross's kiss to allow reality to intrude.

'Sorry to interrupt, Heather, but can you come? We've an RTA on the way—a couple injured when their car overturned.' Abby shot an apologetic glance at Ross. 'I wouldn't have bothered you but Ben is tied up in Resus with a suspected myocardial infarc and Rob isn't up to handling something as serious as this.'

'Of course. I…I'll be right there.' Heather summoned a smile but it was hard not to show her dismay as she came back to earth with a bump. 'I'd better go and see what's happening,' she said huskily after Abby had left. She hurriedly stepped out of Ross's arms and went to the door, feeling her legs trembling as the full enormity of what had happened hit her. How could she have let Ross kiss her like that? How could she have kissed him back that way? How could she have *considered* breaking her own sacred rules?

'We didn't do anything wrong, Heather.'

She paused when Ross spoke, although she couldn't bring herself to look at him in case he could tell how scared she felt. 'Of course not. Now, if you'll excuse me…'

'Dammit, Heather, don't do that!'

The anger in his voice startled her so much that she turned. 'Do what? I don't know what you mean.'

'Don't you? So you aren't deliberately shutting me out, then?' He crossed the room in a couple of long, angry strides and caught hold of her by the shoulders. 'You're willing to swear on the Bible that it *isn't* what you're doing?'

'I don't have to swear to anything!' she shot back, her own anger igniting as quickly as his had done. Maybe it wasn't fair to blame him for what had happened when she'd been such a willing participant, but she couldn't help it. If Ross hadn't kissed her then she wouldn't be in this position. 'Nor do I have to explain myself to you!'

'No, you don't, but it appears that I owe you an explanation, Heather.'

He treated her to a grim smile as he let her go. Heather felt a wave of sickness rise inside her when she saw the bitterness in his eyes. It was obvious that he was deeply hurt by what she'd said, but there was no way she could apologise when it would only make matters worse.

'I made the mistake of thinking that the situation between us had changed but I can see that I was wrong. All I can say is that I never meant to embarrass you.' He opened the door. 'Now I'd better go and check on the boys.'

Heather felt a lump come to her throat as he left the room. It was all she could do not to call him back, but what would be the point? What could she tell him? That she didn't regret letting him kiss her?

She took a deep breath but it was hard to blot out the images that filled her head. It had been such a long time since a man had kissed her the way Ross had done—with such passion, such hunger—that she could feel herself trembling at the memory. Ross had apologised but she knew in her heart that he wasn't the guilty one. She could have stopped him any time she'd chosen but she hadn't wanted to. The truth was that she'd wanted Ross every bit as much as he'd wanted her.

Heather's shift finally came to an end almost an hour after she was due to go off duty. The two car-crash victims had been taken to Theatre. Both had suffered multiple injuries and it had taken a real team effort to get them stable. Heather was as relieved as everyone else when they were finally able to go home. It had been a stressful night one way and another.

She collected her coat and headed for the exit. She had to pass the relatives' room and automatically glanced through the glass pane in the door. Ross was sitting on the sofa with the twins cuddled up at either side of him. The three of them looked so worn out that Heather's footsteps slowed. Maybe Ross wouldn't welcome her interference after what had happened earlier, but she couldn't leave without first checking to see if he needed anything.

She tapped on the door and went in, pinning a smile to her mouth when all three looked up. 'Hi. How are you doing?'

'Heather!' Josh scrambled off the sofa and came running to her.

Heather laughed as she bent and hugged him. 'What a lovely welcome!'

'We missed you, didn't we, Uncle Ross?' Josh said guilelessly, turning to the man sitting on the sofa. Heather's smile slipped when Ross didn't answer. It was obvious that he, at least, wasn't pleased to see her.

'I thought I'd pop in and see if you needed anything before I went home,' she explained hurriedly.

'No, thank you. We're fine,' Ross replied politely.

Heather's heart sank when she heard the chilly note in his voice. Maybe it was silly to let it upset her but she couldn't bear to think that they would part on such bad terms.

'Are you sure?' She felt a little colour wash up her face when he raised a sardonic brow. Ross obviously didn't believe her concern was genuine but *she* knew it was. The thought spurred her on. 'What's going to happen about the boys?'

'They'll have to stay here with me for the time being.' He shrugged. 'Once Mike arrives then we can sort something out.'

Heather looked uncertainly at the twins, who were now kneeling by the coffee-table and listlessly playing a board game. Their faces were grey from lack of sleep and her heart went out to them.

'Do you think it's a good idea to keep them here?' she said quietly so the children couldn't hear. 'They really need to go home to bed.'

'I'm sure you're right, and as soon as Mike gets here, I'll take them home,' Ross said shortly.

'But it could be hours before he arrives!'

'So what do you suggest, Heather? There's no way I can leave here until I know that Kate is going to be all right.'

His tone was curt to the point of rudeness but she guessed

that was because he was worried rather than angry about what
had happened between them. Ross was trying to do his best
for everyone concerned, but it wasn't easy to balance the needs
of his sister against those of his young nephews. Heather came
to a swift decision, even though she wasn't sure if it was wise
to get involved. She couldn't just walk away and leave him to
cope on his own. Her heart wouldn't let her.

'What I suggest is that I take Josh and Luke home with me
and you collect them later. It makes far more sense than keeping them here, don't you think, Ross?'

CHAPTER NINE

ROSS was so stunned by Heather's offer that several seconds must have elapsed before he could speak. 'I don't think that's a good idea…'

'Of course it is!' Heather didn't give him a chance to finish. Ross saw her eyes flash with impatience as she pushed back her cuff and checked her watch. 'It's just gone seven already so what time does your brother-in-law expect to get here?'

'I'm not sure,' he admitted. 'It all depends when Mike can get on a flight to London. Most of the seats will have been booked months ago so he may have to wait for a cancellation.'

He shook his head when she went to say something else. Standing up, he gestured towards the door. He preferred to discuss this out of earshot of the children rather than run the risk of upsetting them if the conversation became too heated. Frankly, the last thing he would have expected Heather to do was to offer to look after the twins after what had happened earlier.

His heart hiccuped as the memory of those magical few minutes he'd spent kissing her came rushing back. It was an effort to put it out of his mind as he explained to the boys that he would just be outside. He followed Heather into the corridor, wondering why it was so important to her that she should be allowed to help him. Exactly what did she hope to achieve by it? He had no idea, but he'd made one mistake that day and he wasn't about to make a second and suffer the consequences.

'Look, Heather, I'm grateful to you for offering to look after the boys but I wouldn't dream of putting on you like that,' he said firmly, determined that he was going to take control of the situation. 'It wouldn't be fair.'

'It isn't fair to the twins to keep them here either,' she retorted. 'They're completely worn out and they need some sleep. I can take them home with me and you can collect them whenever you want to. I really can't see what the problem is.... Unless you don't trust me to look after them,' she added uncertainly.

'Of course I trust you!' He sighed when he saw her jump but he couldn't bear to see her looking so hurt. 'Sorry. I didn't mean to snap but you're crazy to suggest such a thing. I know the twins would be perfectly safe with you, Heather. It just seems too much to expect you to take care of them after you've been working all night.'

'It isn't a problem. Really. I can put the boys to bed then have a sleep myself. Mum is going shopping with Grace so it will be nice and peaceful in the flat.'

'But why do you want to do this?' he countered. 'I don't mean to appear ungrateful but I don't understand why you're so keen to help when you made it clear before that you weren't interested in me or my problems.'

'That isn't true. It isn't that I don't care, Ross. It's just that I'm...well, wary about getting too involved.'

'Taking Josh and Luke home with you entails a certain degree of involvement,' he pointed out.

'I suppose it does, but it's what a friend would do if he or she wanted to help.'

'So what you're saying is that you want us to be friends? Have I got that right?' he asked, wanting to be sure that he wasn't making another mistake.

'Yes, I suppose I am. I...I can't bear to think that you hate me for what I said before, Ross.'

'I could never hate you, Heather,' he admitted huskily. He cleared his throat, realising that he was in danger of saying too much if he didn't get a grip of himself. Now certainly wasn't the time to confess how he really felt about her.

'And you're quite sure you don't mind looking after the boys? Obviously, I'll collect them as soon as I can, but I don't know how long it will be before I can leave here. I want to stay until Kate has come round from the anaesthetic at the very least.'

'It isn't a problem. You can leave them with me for as long as you want to.' She looked at him and smiled. 'I want to help any way I can, Ross, and I mean that.'

Ross felt his heart race when he saw the warmth in her eyes. It was obvious that she was telling him the truth and the knot of pain that had been lodged in his chest for the past hour suddenly began to ease.

'Then all I can say is thank you. I really appreciate this, Heather, especially after...'

He stopped, not wanting to spoil their new-found harmony by harking back to what had happened. It had felt like such a complete and total rejection when Heather had stated that she didn't owe him anything that it had cut him to the quick. But maybe he'd been at fault for expecting too much? Heather had tried to comfort him and he should never have overstepped the boundaries by kissing her.

Only she didn't try to stop you, did she? a small voice whispered. It was only *after* they'd been interrupted that she'd had second thoughts. Maybe she'd realised how deep her feelings really were for him and she'd been scared at the thought of breaking her rule about not getting involved.

Ross's head whirled as he tried to absorb that tantalising thought but it was too much to cope with when he had so many other issues to deal with. He put it to the back of his mind as they went to tell the twins that Heather was going to take them home with her. They seemed perfectly happy with the arrangement, he was relieved to see.

'I'll collect you both later.' Ross bent down and hugged them. 'Just make sure that you're good for Heather, won't you?'

'We will, Uncle Ross,' Luke promised solemnly. He ran to Heather and took hold of her hand and Josh quickly followed suit.

Ross stood up, trying to ignore the tugging on his heart strings as he looked at the three of them standing there. He could just imagine how wonderful it would be to see Heather with *their* children.

'How are you getting home?' he said gruffly, shocked by the speed with which that idea had surfaced. 'You can't take the boys on the tube in their pyjamas.'

'It might cause a bit of a sensation.' Heather laughed as she looked at the twins. 'I suppose we'd better take a taxi, hadn't we, guys?'

'I've a better idea. Do you drive?' Ross quickly hunted his car keys out of his pocket when she nodded. 'Then you can take my car. It will be quicker than trying to find a cab at this time of the morning. Taxis are scarcer than gold dust during the rush-hour.'

'But what about you?' she protested.

'The rush will be over by the time I leave here so I can take a cab.' He offered her the keys and after a slight hesitation she took them. 'Right, I'd better show you where I've parked, hadn't I?'

He opened the door, waiting while Heather led the twins into the corridor. He followed them to the exit then took the lead as they made their way to the car park. Even at that hour of the day there were a lot of vehicles already parked there and he was glad that he hadn't left her to find the car on her own.

Heather unlocked the doors and the twins scrambled into the back. Ross helped Luke with his seat belt while Heather helped Josh fasten his. He opened the door on the driver's side and waited while she slid behind the wheel. Crouching down beside her, he gave her a quick run-through of the controls, wanting to be sure that she was comfortable driving a strange vehicle.

'You're quite happy with everything?' he asked anxiously.

'Fine, although there might be a few kangaroo hops when I set off.' She grinned at him. 'I forgot to mention that it's been some time since I was behind a steering-wheel. I hope you aren't too worried about your clutch.'

'So long as you feel confident about driving it then I don't care what you do,' he declared truthfully.

'Ah, so you're that rare breed, are you? A man who doesn't

mind the odd scratch or two on his paintwork,' she teased, her eyes full of laughter.

'At the end of the day, a car is just a lump of metal and it can be replaced,' he said softly, wondering if she had any idea how adorable she looked. It was rare to see her looking so relaxed and he couldn't help wishing that she did it more often. 'It's people who matter most, Heather. You can't ever replace them.'

'Maybe you shouldn't try,' she whispered with a catch in her voice. Ross felt a searing pain run through him when he saw the shadows in her eyes. He knew immediately that she was thinking about her fiancé. Even after all this time her loss was still so painful that it coloured everything she did.

He stood up and closed the door because he didn't want her to see how much that thought had grieved him. He waved to the twins then made his way back to the hospital because there was no point standing there, wishing for something he couldn't have. If Heather was still in love with the other man then he had to accept that. It didn't mean he had to like the idea but he had to learn to live with it. The trouble was that it might also mean him learning to live without Heather and he wasn't sure he could manage that. It would be like asking him to live without sunshine and fresh air. He could *exist* without them but the world would be a very grey and dreary place.

Heather woke at two, feeling much better for having had several uninterrupted hours of sleep. She pulled on a comfortable old towelling robe over her pyjamas and went to check on the twins. She'd put them in her room and had slept in Sandra's bed, and they were still fast asleep when she popped her head round the door.

She went into the kitchen and made some tea. Her mother had told her that she was going to take Grace to the park after they'd finished their shopping and that it would be mid-afternoon before they got back. Heather decided to take advantage of the extra free time and sat down to enjoy her tea instead of taking it into the bathroom with her as she normally did. She would have plenty of time to shower and dress before they got home.

The thought had barely crossed her mind when she heard a knock on the front door. Heather rushed to the sitting-room window and groaned when she saw Ross standing on the door-step. She didn't need to look in the mirror to know that her hair was hanging in rats' tails around her shoulders and that the tatty old robe looked as though it should have been pensioned off decades ago. How typical that he should arrive when she looked such a sight!

'Hi. I hope I didn't wake you.'

Ross smiled at her when she opened the door. Heather tossed back her hair, knowing that she would just have to brazen it out. Anyway, what difference did it make how she looked? Ross wasn't here to see her; he'd come to collect the twins.

'I'd just got up, actually.' She led the way to the kitchen, trying not to feel self-conscious about the fact that several inches of Winnie the Pooh printed pyjama legs were visible beneath the hem of her robe.

'So I can see. Nice pyjamas, by the way. I used to be a Pooh fan, too, in my younger days.'

The laughter in his voice brought a rush of colour to Heather's cheeks and she busied herself by plugging in the kettle. 'My mother bought them for me for Christmas. Grace loves the books and she chose them when Mum took her shopping for my present.'

'Obviously a child with excellent taste.' Ross pulled out a chair and sank down on it with a sigh. 'Phew, it's been a long night.'

'You must be exhausted,' Heather sympathised, forgetting her embarrassment when she heard the weariness in his voice. 'How's Kate?'

'Still unconscious.' He ran his hands over his face and Heather could hear the dry rasp of stubble beneath his fingers. 'I had a word with her consultant before I left and he told me that the operation had gone as planned. He also said that Kate would be sedated for a while, although I'm not sure why exactly. I was so tired by then that I didn't really take it all in.'

'To minimise the effects of shock,' Heather explained. 'Both the initial injury to the brain and the operation will have caused a degree of trauma so keeping Kate sedated will help her body deal with it. They will gradually reduce the amount of sedatives she receives over the next day or so.'

'And hopefully she will regain consciousness then? Although there's no guarantee, I suppose.'

'Don't think about that now,' she said quickly when she heard the anxiety in his voice. 'Kate has come through the operation and that's the main thing. Now, how about a cup of tea?'

'I don't know if I can stay awake long enough to drink it.' He yawned widely. 'Excuse me! I think I'd better collect the boys and get off home. I need to make arrangements with one of Kate's friends to look after them while I go back to the hospital.'

'Is there no sign of your brother-in-law yet?' Heather asked worriedly. It was obvious how exhausted Ross was and she hated to think of him going straight back to the hospital without taking time to rest.

'Mike phoned me about an hour ago. He's had to make a stop-over in Frankfurt because he couldn't get on a direct flight to London,' he explained. 'Unfortunately, there's been problems with the new air traffic control system and all flights into the UK have been delayed. Mike has no idea what time he will eventually get here.'

'I see. But is there nobody else who could help? Other members of your family who could visit Kate or look after the twins?'

'I'm afraid not. Our parents died some years ago so there's just Kate and me, apart from some distant cousins we never see. Mike is from Canada and his family all live over there.' He shrugged. 'Basically, it's all down to me at the moment.'

'Then it's even more important that you get some rest while

you can,' she said firmly. 'You can't keep going without any
sleep, Ross.'

'I should be able to snatch half an hour when I get back to
the hospital. I can catnap in the visitors' lounge once I've
checked on Kate.'

'You need more than a catnap in a hard hospital chair,' she
protested. The kettle boiled so she made him a cup of tea and
sat down at the table, determined to make him see sense. 'Anyway, the twins are still fast asleep and it doesn't seem fair to
wake them up.'

'I can't leave them with you any longer, Heather. You must
have things to do. I'll take them home as soon as I've drunk
this.'

He took a thirsty swallow of the tea and shuddered appreciatively. 'This tastes so much better than the stuff you get out
of those wretched machines! Heaven knows what they put in
it but it tastes more like stewed sawdust than tea.'

'Tell me about it!' She laughed softly, thinking how handsome he looked despite the fact that he was obviously worn
out. The dark stubble on his jaw gave him a rakish air whilst
the shadows under his hazel eyes made them look even more
soulful than ever. When he pushed back his hair, Heather found
her eyes drawn to the crisp dark strands, loving the way they
immediately sprang back into place....

'Penny for them?'

She jumped when he touched her lightly on the hand, feeling
the ready colour wash up her face when she found him watching her. 'Oh, they're not worth a penny. My head is a complete
muddle until I've had a shower and a second cup of tea.'

'Mmm, I know what you mean. I'm fit for nothing until I've
had my daily dose of caffeine.' He smiled at her, his tired hazel
eyes lingering on her hair. 'Do you know, it's the first time
I've seen you with your hair down? You should wear it like
that more often.'

'It's a mess,' she protested. 'I really should get it cut but I
just never seem to get round to it.'

'It would be a shame to cut it all off.' He lifted a strand off her collar and let it slide through his fingers. 'It feels so won-derfully soft.'

Heather gulped in air when she felt the gentle tugging on her hair but there didn't seem to be any oxygen getting to her lungs. A wave of giddiness assailed her and she hastily pushed back her chair, ignoring the startled look Ross gave her.

'Would you mind if I had a shower while you're here?' she said, using the first excuse that came to mind. Ross had only been touching her hair but he might have been making love to her from the way her heart was pounding!

'I didn't want to run the risk of the boys waking up while I was in the bathroom and not hearing them. They might be frightened if they wake up in a strange place.'

'Of course I don't mind. But are you sure it wouldn't be easier if I took them home?'

'No. Let them sleep a bit longer.' She summoned a smile but it was hard to ignore the way the blood was beating inside her veins. 'Why don't you make yourself another cup of tea and take it into the sitting-room? It will be more comfortable in there.'

'Sounds very tempting,' he conceded. 'If I'm honest, I have to admit that I could do with catching my breath. My feet don't seem to have touched the ground for the past twelve hours. OK, you've convinced me. You go and have your shower, Heather, and I'll have another cup of tea before I drive the boys home.'

He got up to switch on the kettle and Heather quickly moved out of his way. She went straight to the bathroom and turned on the shower, adjusting the dials until a steady stream of hot water flowed from the jets. Stripping off her nightclothes, she stepped under the spray and took a bottle of shower gel off the rack.

She smoothed a handful of scented gel over her wet skin, shivering when her fingers brushed her nipples. Her hand quickly moved on while she spread the gel over her ribs, her waist, the swell of her stomach, and she felt her breathing quicken. All of a sudden she was so deeply aware of her own body that it shocked her. She couldn't recall ever feeling like that before, couldn't remember being conscious of every cell and sinew, every pulse and pleasure point—not even when Stewart had been making love to her.

The plastic bottle slid from her fingers and landed in the shower tray with a noisy thud. Heather didn't even notice. Stewart had been a gentle and considerate lover but he had never really aroused her passion. She had enjoyed their love-making but she hadn't really *missed* it since he'd died. She had missed their closeness, of course, the love and friendship they had shared, but her body had never *ached* because it had been denied the fulfilment only Stewart could have given her. She hadn't really understood what passion truly felt like until Ross had come into her life.

'Heather, are you OK?'

She jumped when Ross rapped on the bathroom door. She quickly turned off the shower and wound a towel around herself. Her hair was dripping down her back, cold rivulets of water trickling down her heated skin and she started shivering as she opened the door a crack.

'I'm fine. Why? What's the matter?'

'I heard a thud and thought you might have slipped....'

His voice tailed off and she heard him swallow. Heather felt her breath catch when she saw his eyes skim from the top of her wet head to the tips of her equally wet feet. She closed her own eyes because the expression on his face was too much to deal with on top of what she'd been thinking moments earlier. Ross wanted her. She could tell that from the lines of strain that were etched on his face, just as she could hear it in the grating sound of his voice as he repeated the question.

'Are you quite sure you're all right, Heather?'

'No. I'm not sure about anything any more, if you want the truth.'

She hadn't meant to say that but the words had slipped out before she could stop them. Her eyes flew open and she stared at him in dismay. She couldn't get involved with Ross! It would be a terrible mistake. So why had she said that to him?

'It's all right. There's no need to be scared, sweetheart. There's nothing to be frightened of.'

He gently pushed open the door. Heather knew she should protest as he stepped into the room but she couldn't find the strength. She backed away as he slowly advanced until she was forced to stop when she felt the coldness of the tiled wall behind her.

'I would never hurt you, Heather,' he said softly as he came to a halt just inches away from her. Reaching out, he tucked a wet strand of her hair behind her ear. 'You know that, don't you?'

Heather shuddered when she felt his fingers brush her cheek. She could feel the heat from them soaking into her skin and was struck by a sudden, desperate yearning to feel that heat in other parts of her body. And in some strange, inexplicable way her need must have communicated itself to him.

Her heart started to race when she felt his fingers glide from her cheek to her jaw. Everywhere Ross touched, Heather could feel her skin burning yet the rest of her felt so cold that there were goose-bumps forming all over her body. She shivered and felt his fingers pause on the throbbing pulse beneath her jaw.

'You can tell me to stop any time you want to, Heather.'

His voice was as deep and as warm as velvet and Heather's senses swam with delight. There was not only his touch to enjoy now but the sound of his voice as well. She let the vibrations from it ripple through her like a musician finely tuning an instrument before a performance, and sighed with pleasure.

'I'll take it that you don't want me to stop, then?'

This time there was tender amusement in his voice as well as velvet and Heather felt a smile tilt up the corners of her mouth.

'Not yet,' she agreed, staring up at him with dreamy grey eyes. She heard him groan deep in his throat and felt a spasm shoot through her when she realised that Ross was every bit as affected by what was happening as she was.

She took a deep breath because the thought had made her head reel and all of a sudden became aware of the delicious mixture of aromas in the steamy bathroom. There was the scent of the shower gel she had used, of course, but its delicate floral fragrance was overlaid by a muskiness that immediately made her drink in another deep lungful of air. She recognised it immediately as Ross's own—the heady, sensual aroma of virile man.

'Pheromones,' she murmured, and heard him laugh softly.

'Bless you! I take it that was the medical equivalent of a sneeze?'

'You could be right.' Heather chuckled, although she couldn't help feeling shocked that they could joke at a time like this. In her admittedly limited experience there was a time for love-making and a time for laughter and the two had never been combined before. But it didn't feel odd when Ross counterbalanced the highly charged atmosphere with lightness. If anything, it enhanced what she was feeling....

A spasm shot through her when Ross's fingers suddenly arrived at her collar-bone and began exploring. Heather felt every single pulse spring to life as he began drawing delicate patterns on her skin, as though he was tattooing her with pleasure. She closed her eyes so that she could better savour the experience by focusing on the feel of his fingers. Sight, hearing and smell were all very well but touch was so much better....

She gasped when he suddenly bent and she felt the warm roughness of his tongue licking the moisture from her skin. Nothing she'd experienced before had prepared her for how deliciously erotic it felt. She tipped back her head to give him even more licence and he took immediate advantage.

His tongue delicately lapped the moisture from her skin from one shoulder to the other then travelled all the way back, sipping, tasting, savouring her flesh as though it was the rarest delicacy. Heather could feel his warm breath cloud on the upper curve of her breasts for a moment before he slowly straightened.

She opened her eyes then and looked at him, knowing she would remember this moment for the rest of her life. It was as though she had finally been initiated into the delights of being a woman. It should have been a ridiculous idea in view of the fact that she had a child, but it was true. For the first time in her life she felt wonderfully, marvellously alive and the realisation filled her with guilt because it seemed like a denial of everything she'd ever felt for Stewart.

Tears filled her eyes and she saw Ross frown in concern. 'What is it? What have I done?'

'You haven't done anything.' It was hard to get the words out but Heather couldn't let him take responsibility when he wasn't at fault. 'It's not you, Ross. It's me. I should never have let things reach this point.'

'How can you say that?' he exclaimed, trying to draw her into his arms.

Heather pushed him away, not because she hated the thought of him holding her but for the opposite reason. She ached to have his arms around her, to feel his hands caressing her and enjoy the pleasure only Ross could give her, but admitting it only made her feel worse. She'd loved Stewart, she really had, but she couldn't lie to herself and pretend that she'd ever felt this way when Stewart had made love to her!

'Please, don't. I'm sorry, Ross…'

'For God's sake, Heather, stop it! Don't do this to yourself or to me.'

He didn't try to touch her again but the pain in his voice was more than enough to gain her attention. Heather's heart ached afresh because it was all her fault that he was suffering.

'Don't push me away again, Heather. Talk to me. Tell me what the problem is and then maybe we can find a solution. I…I know this has something to do with Grace's father and I swear that I'll understand.'

His eyes met hers and she saw the desperation they held. 'Just give me a chance, Heather. That's all I'm asking for—a chance to make you see that your life isn't over.'

CHAPTER TEN

ROSS could feel beads of sweat breaking out on his forehead as he waited for Heather to answer. He knew that he might have ruined everything by asking her to tell him about her past, but he'd had no choice. He couldn't keep on letting her shut him out all the time! They had to confront this issue once and for all—no matter what the outcome might be.

A spasm of terror gripped him at the prospect of never seeing Heather again. In that moment Ross knew there was no way that he could pretend about his feeling any longer. He loved Heather! He wanted her in his life and in his heart from here to eternity, but he had to prepare himself for the fact that she might send him away.

'Heather, please. I know it's a lot to ask but we need to talk about what happened—*you* need to talk about it.'

His tone was as gentle and as reassuring as he could make it, even though his frustration was growing with every second that she remained silent. He wanted to shake her, kiss her, hold her or hug her—do *anything* it took to make her respond—but he couldn't do any of those things. This had to be Heather's decision and he mustn't try to coerce her when she was so vulnerable.

'I…I want to tell you, Ross. It's just that I'm…afraid.'

Her voice was so low that he had to strain to hear her and he frowned as he tried to make sense of what she'd said. 'You mean you're afraid of how I might react, that I might be angry?' he queried, unable to keep the hurt out of his voice. Didn't she realise that he would happily lay down his life rather than hurt her? Apparently not.

'No! I'm afraid of what it will do to me.' She looked up at him and his heart ached when he saw that her eyes were swimming with tears. 'I don't know if I can handle the pain again. That's why I…I never talk about what happened to Stewart—because it's easier.'

'I understand how hard it must be to lose someone you love, sweetheart. But not talking about it doesn't help.' He couldn't stop himself from touching her then because it broke his heart to see her looking so upset. He ran his hands gently down her bare arms and could have wept himself when he felt her flinch.

His hands fell to his sides and it was all he could do to contain his anguish because having her rebuff him seemed like an omen of what was to come. Heather was going to send him away and there wasn't a thing he could do about it.…

'I know I was wrong not to talk about Stewart's death or go for counselling afterwards, but there was Grace to think about. I…I didn't want to run the risk of upsetting her.'

Ross could barely hide his relief when he realised what she'd said. He'd been so afraid that she would tell him to leave. He glanced around the bathroom and spotted her robe hanging on a hook behind the door. Lifting it down, he held it out to her.

'Why don't you put this on then we can go into the sitting-room while we talk?' he suggested, knowing it would be hard to hold a proper conversation while they were standing in the bathroom. 'It will be more comfortable in there.'

'All right.'

Obediently, she unhooked the damp towel from around her and let it fall to the floor so she could slide her arms into the robe. Ross felt a shaft of desire shoot through him when he saw her naked for the very first time. Even the glimpses he'd had so far hadn't fully prepared him for her true beauty.

Her skin had a pearly sheen, the delicate tracery of blue veins across her full breasts simply emphasising how fine it was. Ross was unable to stop himself as his gaze skimmed hungrily down over the neat tuck of her waist, the gentle swell of her hips and belly to the cloud of dark curls nestling between her thighs. He could feel his body responding to her beauty but he knew that he couldn't do a thing about it. It would be wrong to allow his desire to surface when he needed to remain calm.

Heather was going to tell him about her relationship with Grace's father and he must focus on that, but it was hard when his body was clamouring about its needs.

'Let's go into the sitting-room,' he said thickly once she had fastened the belt around her waist. He stepped aside so that she could lead the way, drawing in several deep breaths in the hope that they would calm him down. They worked to a point but he could still feel the throbbing in his groin as he sat down and quickly crossed his legs. He had to put his feelings aside and concentrate on Heather.

'How long ago did Stewart die?' he asked gently once she had settled herself on the sofa with her feet tucked beneath her.

'It's almost three years now.'

'You told me that he'd died before Grace was born,' he prompted when she fell silent.

'That's right. I was six weeks pregnant when Stewart was killed. I'd been to see my GP that very day, in fact, and had had it confirmed.' She sighed. 'I'd done a home pregnancy test but I wanted to be sure before I told Stewart.'

'I expect he was delighted,' Ross said calmly, even though the thought made him feel all churned up. It wasn't hard to imagine *his* delight if Heather announced she was expecting their baby, and it was difficult to deal with the thought that it was unlikely to happen.

'Stewart had no idea that I was expecting his child and that's one of the things I regret most of all. I should have told him as soon as I suspected that I was pregnant, instead of waiting!'

Ross could barely hide his dismay when he heard the anguish in her voice. It was obvious how painful Heather found it to talk about the past and he found himself wondering if he'd been right to press her.

'You mean that Stewart died before you could tell him about the baby?' he asked quietly, because it was too late to have second thoughts.

'Yes. Do you remember that fire that broke out in St Leonard's Hospital?'

'Of course. I was one of the officers who attended.'

Ross frowned as he thought back to what had happened. It had been a major incident, involving crews from a number of fire stations in the Greater London area. He'd been promoted to Station Officer just a few weeks previously and it had been his first real test. He'd been commended for his part in the proceedings, although he had never considered it to be a complete success because there had been one fatality.

'One of the doctors was killed when he was trapped inside the building after rescuing a patient…' He broke off and stared at her in dismay. 'That was your fiancé?'

'Yes. I should have been at work as well but I'd booked the morning off to see my GP. By the time I arrived at the hospital the fire had really taken hold. I just set to and helped out wherever I could. There were hundreds of patients who had to be evacuated and I was kept busy attending to them.

'I'd seen Stewart a couple of times so I knew he was all right, although we hadn't had a chance to speak because it was so chaotic. I had no idea that he'd gone back inside until one of the nurses came to fetch me.…'

She stopped and swallowed. 'The firemen found him in the casualty department. He…he was very badly burnt and never regained consciousness.'

Ross didn't know what to say. He'd seen enough burns victims to imagine how traumatic it must have been for her. He cleared his throat. 'I believe your fiancé was awarded a medal for his bravery. If he hadn't gone back inside then the old lady he rescued would have died.'

'That's right. There was a huge fuss made at the time. Everyone said that Stewart was a hero and that I should be proud of what he'd done, but I couldn't see it that way.'

She ran her hands over her face to wipe away the tears that were streaming down her cheeks. 'All I could think about was that I hadn't told him about the baby and that now he would never know. He wanted a family so much, you see, and I knew he would have been thrilled.…'

Her voice broke and she buried her face in her hands. Ross saw her body heave with sobs and got to his feet. Crossing the room, he crouched in front of her and pulled her into his arms, hating himself for putting her through such an ordeal.

'Shh, darling, it's all right. It's going to be fine, Heather. I'm here and I'll take care of you. I love you so much.'

He rocked her from side to side as he whispered reassurances to her. He had no idea what he was saying but it didn't matter. He just wanted to comfort her and try to make amends for making her relive the nightmare. He had *never* intended to put her through this kind of torment!

'What did you say?'

The shock in her voice cut through his thoughts and Ross abruptly released her. His stomach lurched as he hastily backtracked over what he'd said and he bit back a groan of dismay. He'd just told Heather that he loved her. Now what was he going to do?

Heather's heart was pounding so hard that she could feel its beat making her whole body vibrate. When Ross got up and went to the window it was a relief. Maybe she'd be able to think if he wasn't holding her.

Her mind swooped back to what he'd said and she bit her lip. Ross had said that he loved her, but people said all manner of things when they were trying to comfort one another. It could have been a simple slip of the tongue....

Only she didn't really believe that.

Heather shot to her feet. Oddly enough, the memory of what had happened to Stewart seemed far less painful now than the idea that Ross had fallen in love with her. She couldn't bear to think that she might have to hurt him, but what choice did she have? She certainly couldn't allow herself to fall in love with him...

Could she?

The question made her gasp and she saw him turn. There were deep lines grooved either side of his mouth that hinted at the strain he was under and Heather's heart ached all the more because of what he must be going through. Ross was a proud man and he must hate the thought that he might have made a fool of himself.

'It's easy to get carried away in the heat of the moment,' she said quickly, wanting to give him a way out.

'Very easy. However, that doesn't change how I feel Heather. I love you. I hadn't meant to tell you that but there's no point lying about it.'

'I had no idea…' she began, then stopped because there was no way that she could lie to him either. She'd known that Ross was attracted to her. It was one of the reasons why she'd been so afraid of getting involved with him, that plus the fact that he had aroused such deep feelings in her.

'I suppose I tried not to think about what was happening,' she admitted.

'Because of Stewart?' He sighed. 'I don't really need to ask you that when it's obvious that you've never got over losing him. He must have been quite a guy for you to be so in love with him after all this time.'

'Stewart was a wonderful person and I loved him very much,' she said softly. 'But it's what happened *to* him that affected me most of all. I'm scared of falling in love again, Ross, and going through the same kind of heartache. I don't think I could bear it and I certainly wouldn't want Grace's life to be blighted by another tragedy.'

'But surely you can see that the odds on it happening again are minute?'

'Maybe, but my life fell apart after Stewart was killed. I didn't want to carry on living and the thought of ever going back to feeling like that is too much to bear.' She smiled sadly. 'I expect you think I'm a coward, don't you?'

'No,' he said thickly. 'I think you are a very brave and wonderful woman, Heather.'

Heather felt her throat close up when she saw the tears in his eyes. When he held out his arms to her she didn't hesitate. She slid her arms around his waist, held him just as tightly as he held her. She could feel the heavy thudding of his heart beneath her breasts and its thundering beat filled her with sudden hope.

With every powerful beat Ross was telling her that he loved

her, with every breath he took he was saying how much he needed her. He was so brave and strong that it made her wonder if he had enough courage for both of them. Maybe they could make this work if she could draw on his strength.

Heather's own heart started racing. It was such a huge step to take and she wasn't sure that she could manage to overcome her fears. But the thought of not having Ross in her life was more than she could bear. Maybe she wasn't prepared to admit that she loved him just yet but given time…

'Why are you hugging Heather, Uncle Ross? Is she your girlfriend?'

They both sprang apart when they heard a piping little voice coming from the doorway. Heather blushed when she saw Luke and Josh watching them with undisguised interest. Ross muttered something under his breath and she bit back a gurgle of laughter at his obvious embarrassment at having his nephews catch him out.

'Hi, guys. I see you're awake at last,' he said with forced cheerfulness. 'I bet you're both starving so how do you fancy stopping off at the drive-through burger bar on our way home?'

'*Is* Heather your girlfriend, Uncle Ross?' Luke wasn't about to be sidetracked by the promise of food. 'Mummy said it was 'bout time you found a proper girlfriend and settled down.'

'Did she indeed? Remind me to have a word with her.' Ross couldn't hide his discomfort and Heather burst out laughing.

'Remember that saying about out of the mouths of babes.'

'Are you and Uncle Ross going to get married?' Josh obviously decided it was time he added his ten pence worth to the discussion. He smiled angelically at Heather. 'That would mean your little girl would be our sister, wouldn't it?'

'No, it wouldn't, dummy! Mummy's new baby is our sister,' Luke corrected scornfully, mercifully saving her from having to think up an answer. 'Heather's little girl will be our… What will she be, Uncle Ross?'

'I've no idea but it's high time I took you two home and let Heather have some peace and quiet.'

Ross strode across the room and briskly ushered the boys

into the hall, sighing when Josh explained that he needed to go to the bathroom. 'I suppose you'd both better go, but be quick.' He waited until the twins were out of earshot then turned to Heather and grimaced.

'Sorry about that. I don't know where they get their ideas from.'

'I suppose it's logical, really. They saw you holding me and put two and two together.'

'Mmm, but we all know where that can lead. It's easy to add things together and end up with a wrong answer.'

There was a note in his voice which told her that it had been more than a passing comment. 'Meaning what exactly?'

'That I don't want you coming up with any wrong answers, Heather. Just because I've admitted how I feel about you, it doesn't mean that I expect you to feel the same.'

He didn't say anything more as the boys came racing back. Heather bent and hugged them, relieved that she hadn't needed to reply. Undoubtedly, Ross had been right to warn her not to get carried away but she couldn't ignore what had happened. Ross had told her that he loved her—what woman could ignore a declaration like that?

Her heart seemed to swell to double its normal size at the thought so that it was hard to act naturally as she showed them out. Ross paused on the step as the boys dashed down the path. 'Thanks again for looking after them, Heather. I really appreciate it.'

'It was my pleasure,' she said sincerely.

'It wasn't too dreadful for you?' he asked softly.

'No,' she replied, knowing that he hadn't been alluding to her looking after the twins. 'It's time I tried to deal with what happened to Stewart.'

'But don't push yourself too hard. Promise?'

'Promise.' She smiled up at him, loving the way his eyes had filled with concern. It was proof of just how much Ross cared about her. When he bent and dropped a kiss on her lips she had to stop herself clinging to him.

'I'll have to go before the natives get restless,' he said lightly

as he straightened, but Heather could hear the breathy note in
his voice and knew that he'd found it just as hard to break the
contact.

'Maybe I'll see you at the hospital later,' she suggested.

'I'll look forward to it.'

With one last light kiss on her cheek he turned and strode
down the path. Heather waited while he got the twins settled
in the back seat. He beeped the horn in a brief farewell and
drove away.

Heather was just about to shut the door when she saw her
mother and Grace crossing the road. She held out her arms as
Grace came hurtling towards her, lifting the little girl up into
the air and swinging her round.

'More swings,' Grace clamoured when she stopped.

'Later, darling. We'll both be dizzy if I don't stop now.'

'Was that Ross driving away?' Sandra asked, walking up the
path.

'Yes, he came to pick up the boys.' Heather carried Grace
inside and unzipped her coat. 'Did you have a lovely time at
the park, sweetheart?'

'Went on woundabout,' Grace informed her, dragging her
arms out of the coat sleeves.

'Roundabout,' Heather automatically corrected. She hung the
coat on a peg and smiled at her daughter. 'Sounds as though
you had fun.'

'Uh-huh!' Grace ran down the hall and disappeared into the
sitting room and a moment later Heather heard the sound of
toys being emptied from the toy box.

'I don't know where she gets her energy from,' Sandra remarked, hanging up her jacket. 'Roast chicken for tea. I'll just
pop it in the oven.'

'Lovely,' Heather murmured.

She took a deep breath as her mother hurried away. She'd
worked hard to create a stable life for Grace. She'd told herself
that she was content so long as her daughter was safe and
happy, but the situation had changed now that Ross had admitted he loved her. Whether she would be brave enough to

return his feelings was still in question, but she hoped so. Letting herself love Ross would heal the wounds from the past and open up the future for her. She could have everything she'd ever dreamt about if she could only find the courage to put her fears behind her at last.

Ross arranged for the twins to stay the night with one of their friends. He got them dressed and packed a bag with clean nightclothes. Normally, the boys enjoyed sleeping over at Jeremy's house but they weren't happy about being left that day. It was difficult to make them understand why they couldn't go with him to see their mother. Ross knew that Kate would still be attached to the monitoring equipment and he didn't want to risk scaring them. As he drove to the hospital, he found himself wondering if he should ask Heather to have a word with them. She seemed to have the gift of setting their minds at rest.

He sighed as he drove in through the hospital's main gates. Using the twins as an excuse to see Heather was beyond the pale. He needed to give her some space after what had happened. The last thing he wanted was for Heather to feel…well, *pressured* into returning his feelings.

He parked the car and made his way to the intensive care unit. It was shortly before five and the same staff nurse was on duty. She smiled when she saw him. 'Ah, Mr Tanner, I've been trying to get hold of you but your phone was switched off.'

'I must have forgotten to switch it on when I left here,' he exclaimed, feeling fear grip him. 'There's nothing wrong with Kate, is there?'

'No, your sister is fine.' The nurse smiled reassuringly. 'Your brother-in-law has arrived and I thought I might be able to save you a journey if you knew he was here.'

'That was kind of you,' Ross said shakily. 'I wasn't expecting Mike to get here so soon. He told me there were problems with the air traffic control system.'

'So I believe. Anyway, Mr Lawrence is with your sister at

the moment so if you'd wait in the lounge, I'll let him know you're here. We can only allow one visitor per bed, I'm afraid.'

'I understand, but, please, don't disturb him. I expect he'll want to spend some time alone with Kate.'

Ross glanced round as another visitor arrived. Mike's arrival had taken some of the pressure off him and he couldn't help feeling relieved. He decided that he may as well take a break and turned to the nurse again.

'I'll go and have a cup of coffee. Will you tell Mike that I'll be back later?'

Ross left the intensive care unit and made his way downstairs but instead of going into the café, he went outside instead. A fine mist of rain was falling now but he was barely aware of it as he walked down the drive. So much had happened in the past couple of days that it was difficult to think clearly. One minute his life had been going along as normal and the next it had been in chaos.

What had Heather said to him once about the unexpected happening? She'd been right. The worst thing was that now he understood why she'd said that. Her life had fallen into complete disarray after her fiancé had been killed so tragically. No wonder she was afraid of falling in love again, especially with a man like him who lived with danger on a daily basis.

Ross groaned because that thought had struck like a knife between his shoulder blades. He loved Heather but would it be right to risk her happiness by letting her love him in return? What if something happened to him? Could he bear to think that he might be responsible for shattering her life a second time?

He looked back at the hospital and there was an ache in his heart because he knew the answer to every one of those questions. He couldn't and wouldn't do anything to hurt Heather, and if that meant him walking away from her then he would have to find the strength to do so.

It was another busy night in the accident and emergency unit. Heather was run off her feet from the moment she arrived.

There was no chance of her slipping away to see Ross because Ben had phoned in sick again. It meant there was only Rob to share the workload and he wasn't up to dealing with anything too serious.

Heather delegated all the minor problems to him—the cuts and bruises and simple sprains—while she dealt with the more serious cases. There was no time to take a break so she made do with a cup of tea in between seeing patients.

'I don't know where they're all coming from,' Abby declared, adding another patient's name to the whiteboard. 'It's never usually this busy on a Thursday night.'

'Maybe we'll have an easy night tomorrow,' Heather suggested, blowing on her tea to cool it. She felt her heart jolt as she remembered how Ross had done the same thing not long ago—blown on her tea to cool it. It made her feel all warm and tingly just to think about it.

'Oh, it must be love!' Abby grinned when Heather looked blankly at her. 'When was the last time we were slack on a Friday night?'

'I'm not sure,' she replied cautiously. 'It's usually one of our busiest times.'

'Exactly! Which means you would need to be so much in love that your brain cells are scrambled to suggest that we might, *quote* "have an easy night tomorrow".' Abby folded her arms across her ample bosom. 'So who's the lucky man, then, Heather? Or do I really need to ask that after what I witnessed this morning in the office?'

'I don't know what you're talking about,' Heather said, blushing.

'No? So I didn't catch you and the delectable Ross Tanner in a passionate clinch?'

'I was just trying to comfort him,' Heather replied shortly. 'He was upset about his sister.'

'Ah, I see. That explains it. You were showing him due concern and sympathy, just as you would for any relative? I suppose that's why you took his nephews home with you, was it? Because you felt it was your duty as a caring professional?'

'How did you know I took the boys home?' Heather exclaimed. 'You'd already gone by the time I left here.'

'That's true but Mel saw you. Her boyfriend's car had broken down outside and they were waiting for the mechanic to arrive. She saw you driving off with the twins in Ross Tanner's car.'

'I thought Mel was keen on Ben so how come she's going out with someone else?' Heather said quickly, trying to steer the conversation away from herself because it made her feel uncomfortable to know that people were speculating about her and Ross. Her heart gave the oddest little hiccup because the words 'her and Ross' had felt so wonderful.

'Mel's view is simple. If Ben isn't interested then there's plenty of men who are. She certainly doesn't intend to sit at home moping.' Abby smiled kindly. 'Maybe you should take a leaf out of Mel's book. You can't grieve for ever, Heather, no matter how much you loved someone.'

The phone rang and Abby answered it. Heather hurriedly finished her tea then paid a visit to the loo before she saw her next patient. She sighed when she saw how strained she looked as she caught sight of herself in the mirror over the basin as she washed her hands. Was Abby right? Should she have tried harder to get over Stewart's death?

For the first time in years it felt as though there were question marks instead of full stops, possibilities instead of finalities. Ross had told her that he loved her and it had opened the way to so much, but she had to be sure about what she was doing. Ross did a highly dangerous job and she had to be certain she could deal with the constant fear that something might happen to him.

She frowned. And yet what was the alternative? Could she really imagine telling him that she didn't want to see him again and spending the rest of her life regretting what she had done? All of a sudden that thought was far more scary than any other.

CHAPTER ELEVEN

'I CAN'T thank you enough for everything you've done, Ross.'

'I was glad to help. So long as Kate is all right, that's all that matters.' Ross clapped his brother-in-law on the shoulder. They were in the visitors' lounge, taking a break after spending the night at Kate's bedside. Ross had insisted that they should take it in turns to sit with her because Mike had been worn out after his long journey. However, the good news was that Kate was now stable enough to be taken off sedatives and they were currently waiting for her to wake up.

Ross looked up when one of the nurses popped her head round the door. She laughed when both men shot to their feet.

'No need to panic. It's good news. Mrs Lawrence is awake. She's a bit woozy from the medication but she's demanding to see her baby and that's definitely a good sign.'

'Thank heavens for that!' Ross exclaimed in relief. He briskly steered his brother-in-law towards the door. 'Off you go, then. Give Kate my love and tell her that I'll see her later. And tell her not to worry about the twins because I've got everything under control.'

'I will. Thanks, Ross.' Mike looked as though a huge weight had been lifted off his shoulders as he hurried after the nurse.

Ross picked up his sweater and left. It was just after six a.m. and the night staff were going off duty. When the lift reached his floor it was packed so he used the stairs instead. He paused when he reached the ground floor. He'd deliberately not sought Heather out because he still hadn't decided what he should do, but the thought of going home without seeing her was more than he could bear. He veered off towards the accident and emergency unit and laughed when he rounded a bend in the corridor and saw her coming towards him.

'I was just coming to find you. Did you have a good night?' he asked, unable to keep the warmth out of his voice. Maybe he needed to think about their involvement but he couldn't deny that seeing her had made his heart sing.

'Busy.' She returned his smile and Ross felt his heart lift when he saw the pleasure in her eyes. It was obvious that Heather was just as pleased to see him. 'It was non-stop all night, which is why I didn't get a chance to come and see you. How is your sister? Has there been any change?'

'There has. Kate's recovered consciousness and I'm keeping my fingers crossed that she is going to be all right.'

'Why that's marvellous news, Ross!' she exclaimed in delight. 'You must be so relieved.'

'I am. Mike finally got here, too. He's with Kate at the moment, which is why I decided to go home.' He grimaced as he ran his hand over his stubbly chin. 'I need a shower and a shave before I collect the boys from their friend's house.'

'It should take some of the burden off you now that your brother-in-law is home,' she suggested, walking back with him along the corridor.

'It will. Obviously, Kate won't be leaving hospital just yet so Mike will still need a hand, but I should be able to go into work next week. I've been off duty so it hasn't been a problem, but I would have felt really bad if I'd had to leave everyone in the lurch.'

'I'm sure your colleagues would have understood,' she protested. 'Still, it isn't a problem now.'

They left the building and Heather paused to draw in a deep breath of fresh air. 'Oh, does that smell good. I feel as though I've been breathing pure antiseptic all night long! Thank goodness I'm off duty this weekend.'

'What you need is a day out in the country,' Ross suggested, struggling to keep a grip on himself. She looked so lovely as she stood there with her face tilted up to the morning sun that he ached to pull her into his arms and make mad, passionate love to her.

'Is that an offer?' she said softly, turning to look at him.

'If you want it to be,' he said equally quietly. He took hold of her hands, lacing his fingers through her slender ones as he drew her to him and planted a kiss on the tip of her nose. 'I could drive us out to the country tomorrow and we could spend the whole day there if you fancy it.'

'I'd love to but there's Grace and the twins to consider,' she pointed out. 'Your brother-in-law will want to spend time with Kate and I see too little of Grace as it is.'

'We'll take them with us. I expect they will enjoy a day out every bit as much as we shall,' he said quickly, inwardly sighing because he really shouldn't be trying to persuade her to spend any more time with him. He needed to weigh up the pros and cons of letting them get more deeply involved but it was hard to resist the thought of them enjoying a whole day together.

'It would be lovely,' she said wistfully. 'It's been ages since I spent a whole day away from the city. I keep meaning to take Grace out for the day but all I can seem to manage is a trip to the park so she can play on the swings.'

'Then it's about time you had a proper outing,' Ross declared. After all, what harm could there be in them enjoying an outing together when they would have the children with them? 'Why don't I drive you home now and pick you up tomorrow morning around nine? The traffic shouldn't be too horrendous because it's Saturday. I'll try to think of somewhere quiet to take you so the kids can play.'

'That would be lovely if you're sure you don't mind me being a bit groggy,' she agreed, laughing up at him. 'I tend to be a bit spaced out after I've come off nights.'

'So long as you can manage to find your way to the car there won't be a problem. Right, that's all sorted now so let's get you home.'

Ross looped his arm around her shoulders as they went down the steps. He could feel their hips bumping together as they walked and tried to close his mind to the images that tried to invade it. Letting himself remember how beautiful Heather had looked yesterday morning certainly wouldn't help him behave in a manner befitting the time and the place. There were a lot of people about—mainly staff who were going off duty—and Heather wouldn't welcome him making a spectacle of her. Nevertheless, each time he felt the gentle pressure of her hip another spasm of desire shot through him so that he was hard-pressed to keep his hands off her.

Frankly, he was a bundle of nerves by the time they reached her home. Heather turned as he stopped the car and Ross bit back a groan when he saw the light in her eyes. Heather was every bit as aware of him as he was of her! How could any red-blooded man be expected to behave with decorum in this situation?

'Thank you for the lift,' she said, and her voice sounded so sweet and husky that the hairs on the back of his neck stood up.

'You're welcome,' he grated, struggling to keep a grip on himself because they were parked in the middle of a busy street. He might have succeeded, too, if she hadn't leant across the seat and kissed him on the cheek.

Ross didn't hesitate as he turned and captured her mouth, kissed her back with a hunger he didn't attempt to hide. He loved her so much that he didn't give a damn who might be watching them!

'I'd better go.' There was a shaky note in her voice that told him more than any words could have done how she felt.

Ross captured her hand and pressed it, palm down, against his racing heart. 'I'll see you tomorrow. Sleep tight, sweetheart.'

'You, too.' She gently withdrew her hand and opened the car door then stopped. Ross was already reaching for her before she turned. This time their kiss was so hot and wild, so full of promise that he groaned aloud. It was pure agony to let her go again but she needed to sleep and he needed to collect the twins.

Their lips clung for another hungry second before he finally released her. Heather didn't say a word as she got out of the car but he understood why. It must be difficult for her to deal with how she felt when she'd taken such care to safeguard her emotions for the past few years.

His heart was suddenly heavy as he started the engine and drove home. He showered and changed then sat on the sofa until it was time to fetch the boys. Closing his eyes, he let his mind drift where it chose and wasn't surprised when it ended up back with Heather.

She was such a vital part of his life that he couldn't imagine being without her now. He loved her so much but love brought with it many responsibilities. He would never risk hurting her, never take the chance of breaking her heart.

Ross opened his eyes because there was no point trying to blind himself to the truth. The greatest test of his love for Heather might be letting her go.

Heather was awake bright and early the following morning. Normally, she had problems sleeping after she'd come off night duty. It took a day or so for her body to adjust but she'd fallen asleep as soon as her head had touched the pillow. She felt relaxed and refreshed as she showered and dressed in jeans and a snug-fitting grey T-shirt then went to make herself some tea before Grace woke up. It was a beautiful sunny morning and she could see acres of clear blue sky when she peered out of the window. It appeared they'd have a nice day for their trip to the country.

'You're an early bird,' Sandra exclaimed, coming into the kitchen in her dressing-gown. Sandra had gone out to dinner with David Harper the previous evening so Heather hadn't had a chance to tell her mother about her plans. She felt suddenly shy at the prospect of explaining she was spending the day with Ross.

'You're usually dead to the world after you've come off nights,' Sandra continued, popping tea bags into the pot. 'How come you're so bright-eyed and bushy tailed this morning?'

'It's too nice a day to waste it by lying in bed,' Heather said quickly, then frowned when she heard Sandra chuckle. 'What's wrong?'

'You never were any good at telling fibs, Heather. Come along, now, tell me the real reason why you're looking so much more like your old self this morning.'

'My old self. What do you mean?' Heather stared at her mother and heard Sandra sigh.

'That it's been an awfully long time since I saw a sparkle in your eyes, darling. I can't begin to tell you how good it is to see you looking so *alive* for once.' Sandra looked her squarely in the eyes. 'I hope this means that you are finally coming to terms with Stewart's death.'

Heather sank onto a chair. Her legs felt like rubber all of a sudden and there was a panicky feeling inside her. 'I don't know how I feel, if you want the truth, Mum.'

'It's understandable,' Sandra said gently, pouring tea into two mugs and putting them on the table. 'You've been bottling up your emotions for so long that it won't be easy to let go, but you have to be brave, darling. Stewart wouldn't have wanted you to waste your life and you know that, don't you? He would have wanted you to find happiness again.'

'But what if the same thing happens again? What if I fall in love with someone else and he dies, too? I…I don't think I could go through that kind of pain again, Mum.'

'Stewart's death was a tragic accident,' Sandra protested. 'It's highly unlikely that anything like it would happen again.'

'Maybe. But what if the person you love does a job that constantly puts him in danger?' Heather took a shuddering breath because voicing her fears out loud seemed to make them even more real. 'I don't know if I could live with that sort of strain.'

'Does this have anything to do with Ross Tanner?' Sandra said quietly.

'He told me that he loves me, Mum,' Heather whispered.

'And how do you feel about him?' Sandra squeezed Heather's hand when she didn't answer. 'Do you love him, darling?'

'I don't know…. I'm not sure how I feel.'

'Because you're afraid of what it could mean?' Sandra held

her hand tightly when Heather nodded. 'I understand, darling, and I wish I could help you, but only you can decide how you feel. All I can say is that Ross seemed like a really nice man when I met him. And it's obvious Grace likes him, too.'

'She does.' Heather summoned a smile. 'It's not often that she takes to people the way she seems to have taken to Ross, is it?'

'No, it isn't. Maybe you should take that as a positive sign.'

'Maybe.' Heather looked up when she heard her daughter shouting for her. 'Sounds as though her ladyship is awake. Ross is taking us to the country for a day out. He's bringing his nephews along and they should be here just after nine.'

'Good. It's about time you got out and enjoyed yourself.' Sandra picked up her tea. 'I'm having a day out, too, as it happens. David is taking me to Henley for lunch.'

'Dinner last night and lunch today! Do I detect a hint of romance in the air?' Heather teased.

'I certainly haven't ruled it out,' Sandra declared, blushing. She sighed wistfully. 'I hope you won't rule it out either, Heather.'

Heather just smiled before she went to fetch Grace. It would be wrong to make a hasty decision. She had to be sure that she loved Ross as much as he loved her.

Her heart lifted as though it had suddenly sprouted wings because the thought of Ross loving her was so wonderful. If she held fast to that idea then maybe it would help her find the courage to face the future. Her mother had been right because Stewart wouldn't have wanted her to grieve for ever. He definitely wouldn't have wanted her to spend the rest of her life looking back.

His death had been a tragic accident, brought about because he'd been unprepared for the situation he had faced. But Ross used his expertise and experience to counterbalance the danger. And that made a world of difference.

Ross arrived bang on time to collect her. Heather opened the door, putting out a restraining hand when Grace tried to rush past her.

'She's so excited,' she explained, feeling her pulse leap
when she saw how good Ross looked in snug-fitting denim
jeans teamed with a navy-blue polo shirt.

'She isn't the only one,' he declared, his hazel eyes skim-
ming over her like loving hands.

Heather blushed because she could tell he was taking note
of the fact that she was wearing her hair down that day and
had even applied a little make-up. It wouldn't be difficult for
him to work out why she had wanted to look her best.

Ross lifted Grace into his arms when she clamoured to be
picked up but his eyes never left Heather. 'The twins are really
excited and I'm starting to feel a bit like that myself,' he murmured, bending so he could brush a kiss over her mouth.

Heather felt her stomach muscle knot when she felt the
warmth of his lips. She couldn't stop herself from reaching out
to touch him. Her fingers slid into the crisp hair at the nape of
his neck and her breathing quickened when she felt the tip of
his tongue probing her mouth for a second before he pulled
away.

'Mmm, that was nice but we mustn't forget that we have an
audience.' He glanced back at the car and groaned when he
saw two interested little faces peering out of the window. 'Prepare yourself for all sorts of awkward questions! If only the
boys were still Grace's age.'

Heather laughed shakily as she ran a hand over her daughter's dark curls. 'It won't be long before Grace is at the what
and why stage.'

'Which means we should enjoy ourselves while we can,
doesn't it?'

His tone was light enough but Heather was aware of the
undercurrent it held. She just smiled because it would be wrong
to be too hasty making any promises. Ross might be wondering
if she'd reached a decision about her feelings for him but she
needed to be sure before she said anything.

She looked round in relief when Sandra suddenly appeared,

and gasped when her mother handed her a laden picnic basket. 'When did you make all this?'

'While you were getting Grace ready.' Sandra smiled at her. 'It's not very exciting, I'm afraid. Just cheese and ham sandwiches, some cake and fruit…'

'It's wonderful!' Heather kissed her. 'Thanks, Mum. You're a star!'

'You just have a wonderful time.' Sandra turned to Ross and Heather saw a look pass between them. 'Take care of them both, won't you? They're very precious.'

'I shall.' Ross kissed Sandra's cheek and his voice seemed deeper than ever when he continued. 'You can rest assured that they will be perfectly safe with me, Sandra.'

Heather frowned. She wasn't sure what she'd heard in his voice but there had been something—a note of sadness, almost…

She briskly shrugged off that idea and turned to unhook their coats from the rack. 'It might rain,' she explained when Ross's brows rose.

'No way. It's not going to rain on our parade because I won't let it!' He took the coats from her and handed them to Sandra then led Heather to the car. 'You can stow that basket in the boot while I get Grace strapped in. I managed to find one of the car seats the boys used to use when they were small. Grace will be safer in that.'

'Thank you.' Heather was deeply touched by his thoughtfulness. She quickly stowed the basket in the boot, grinning to herself when she discovered the hamper that was already in there. There was also a cricket bat and a ball, some fishing nets and a couple of jamjars with string tied around them for makeshift handles. Ross had obviously come well prepared for their day out.

Grace was obviously delighted to be sitting in the back with the twins. She was chattering away to them in baby talk when Heather got into the car. Heather grinned as Ross started the engine. 'Looks as though we're all ready for off, then.'

'Looks like it.' He turned to the children. 'Who wants to go for a picnic?'

'We do!' the twins chorused, and Grace enthusiastically added her voice.

'What a din!' Heather laughed as she put her hands over her ears. 'I'm beginning to wonder if this was such a good idea after all!'

'Have faith,' Ross declared. 'When have I ever let you down?'

'Never,' she said softly, and there was a lump in her throat all of a sudden. She looked at him with all the pent-up emotion she'd tried to keep in check clearly visible in her eyes. 'You've never let me down, Ross, and you never will.'

'Heather, I—' He half leant towards her then stopped when there was a groan of disgust from the rear seat.

'You and Heather aren't going to start all that *kissing* stuff again, are you, Uncle Ross?'

Ross rolled his eyes as he straightened and glanced in the rear-view mirror. 'Not when there's a picnic about to take place. So, are you ready? Are you steady? Then shall we—?'

'Go!' the boys roared in response to what was obviously a familiar routine.

Heather settled back as Ross pulled away from the kerb. There was a strange feeling of peace stealing over her, a sense of inevitability. She knew that after the day was over she would have made her decision.

'I should have known it was tempting fate!'

Ross dropped the rug onto the floor of the wooden hut. It had begun to rain almost as soon as they had started unloading the car.

Fortunately, he'd decided to take them to a country park and there were a number of shelters dotted about. He'd sent Heather and the children on ahead while he'd followed on with the picnic things, not wanting them to get soaked. Now he grimaced as he patted his damp T-shirt and a shower of raindrops scattered everywhere.

'Remind me to mind my own business the next time you decide to bring a coat with you, Heather.'

'It would have stopped me getting soaked,' she said sweetly, grinning at him.

'All right, there's no need to crow. One "I told you so" will be quite sufficient, thank you very much.'

'All right, then, I told you so,' she retorted impishly.

Ross chuckled when he saw the amusement on her face. 'You're enjoying every second of this, you wretched woman!'

'I have no idea what you mean,' she declared loftily. 'Who in his—or *her*—right mind would enjoy having their picnic rained off?' She cast a speaking look at the rain that was pouring down outside the hut.

Ross sighed. 'It's such a shame, isn't it? And I thought I'd found us the perfect place to spend the day.'

'You did,' she said quickly. 'It's a lovely spot, Ross. There's the river to catch tiddlers in and a field to play ball and somewhere to shelter until the rain stops. We're glad we came, aren't we kids?'

There was a chorus of agreement which made him feel a lot better. Hunkering down on his heels, he spread the rug over the splintery wooden floor and started to unpack the food. 'Then let's carry on enjoying ourselves. We'll have an early lunch and hope that the rain has stopped by the time we finish eating.'

Heather knelt on the rug and helped him unpack their picnic, exclaiming in surprise when she saw the pots of pâté, the sliced meats and bowls of salad he had brought. 'This is a real feast, not just a picnic! You're spoiling us, Ross.'

'It was the easy option,' he admitted, unwrapping some of Sandra's home-made fruit cake. 'I just went to the nearest deli and bought what I thought we'd need.'

'Well, we seem to have something to cater for everyone's taste.' She handed Grace a cheese sandwich which her mother had prepared then helped Josh spoon some exotic-looking pasta salad onto a paper plate. 'We certainly won't go hungry.'

The boys wolfed down their food then began playing a noisy

game of I Spy. Grace was determined to join in even though she really didn't understand what was happening. Ross sighed as he leant against the rough wooden wall and helped himself to another slice of fruit cake.

'Do you think your mother would marry me? I haven't tasted cake this good in years!'

'Sorry, I'm afraid she's spoken for.' Heather grinned as she helped herself to another scoop of pâté and liberally spread it on a cracker. 'Mum has been seeing someone for a few weeks now and it seems to be getting serious.'

'And how do you feel about that?' Ross shrugged when she looked at him in surprise. 'I know how much you rely on your mother to help you with Grace so I just wondered if you were worried that it might complicate things if she remarried.'

'I haven't thought about it.' She bit her lip and frowned. 'I would hate Mum to think that she had to put me and Grace before her own happiness. It wouldn't be fair. I must make that clear to her.'

Ross felt his heart swell with love. 'Have I told you how wonderful I think you are?'

'Not for a while you haven't.' She laughed. 'Although I'm not sure what I've done to deserve such a fulsome compliment.'

'The list is too long and I'm too full of good food to recite it all,' he declared. 'But how about your unselfishness, for starters? You put everyone first, Heather—Grace, your mother, the people you treat in work. Your needs come way down your list of priorities.'

'Maybe that's because I've not allowed myself to think about my own needs for a very long time.' She put the cracker on her plate and rubbed her hands down her jeans in a nervous little gesture that touched his heart. 'It's easier to think about other people than it is to worry about yourself.'

'I know. I understand that, sweetheart.'

Ross felt a knot form in his throat. All of a sudden his stomach was churning and his palms were damp. He'd vowed that he would wait until he had fully considered the consequences of their relationship but he was only flesh and blood! He wouldn't be human if he didn't ache to know if Heather had reached a decision about him, yet at the same time he was terrified of asking in case she told him something he didn't want to hear.

'Ross, there's something I want to say to you.'

Every nerve in Ross's body reacted to the announcement so that he almost leapt ten feet into the air. It felt as though a naked flame had been applied to gunpowder because there seemed to be explosions going off all over his body. His ears were ringing, his heart was hammering and his breathing was so laboured that it actually *hurt*. For the first time in his life he thought he was going to pass out, and gritted his teeth.

No matter what Heather said, he would accept it. He certainly wasn't going to say anything that might make her feel guilty. If she'd decided that she felt nothing for him then he would accept it with dignity. And maybe it would be for the best, too, because he still wasn't sure it would be wise…

'I think—no, I'm *sure*—that I'm falling in love with you, Ross.'

CHAPTER TWELVE

HEATHER bit her lip when she felt a bubble of hysterical laughter rising inside her. The expression on Ross's face was just so comical. It was obvious that he hadn't been expecting her to say that and who could blame him? *She'd* had no idea she was going to come out with that statement.

Her heart performed a somersault as the full impact of what she'd done hit her. She'd just told Ross that she was falling in love with him! It was true, too. Now that she had stopped trying to keep her emotions under wraps it was perfectly clear how she felt.

'I don't know what to say… I can't really believe… It's too much to take in…'

Ross kept starting a sentence and not finishing it but Heather understood how much of a shock this must have been for him because it had been a shock for her, too. Her heart filled with warmth when she saw the bewilderment in his eyes.

'I shouldn't have sprung it on you like that, Ross. I wasn't planning to. It…well, it just sort of came out, if you know what I mean.'

'I do.' He gave a husky laugh as he captured her hand and held it tightly. 'It's not easy to hide your feelings, is it?'

'A week ago I'd have argued with you about that but I wouldn't dream of doing so now,' she admitted. 'I never had any difficulty hiding my feelings in the past, Ross. It's ever since you came onto the scene that it's become a problem.'

'And how does that make you feel?' He ran his thumb over the back of her hand and Heather shivered when she felt the gentle caress.

'Scared, I suppose. I know it's stupid but I'm still afraid that something could go wrong again.' She felt her stomach lurch when she saw the pain that crossed his face. 'Ross, what is it? What did I say?'

'Nothing. I'm just having a hard time taking it all in.' He smiled but she couldn't fail to see the troubled light in his eyes as he leant forward and kissed her.

Grace came running over to them just then and Ross quickly got up and began clearing away the remains of their picnic. Heather put her arms round the little girl, suddenly needing the warmth of the child's sturdy little body. She couldn't explain it but there was a cold feeling inside her, a sense of having made a mistake by declaring her feelings. But Ross had told her that he loved her, she reminded herself. So how could it have been a mistake to tell him how *she* felt?

It was impossible to answer that question so it was a relief to have to deal with what Grace was trying to tell her. Heather laughed when she saw her daughter pointing towards the door. 'Ah, it's stopped raining, has it, and you want to go out and play?'

'Please, Mummy,' Grace said eagerly. She looked at the twins who were squabbling about who had won the most points in their game of I Spy. 'Boys come?'

'We'll all go,' Ross declared, fastening the lid on the hamper. 'I'll just put this in the car and fetch the fishing nets. We can do a spot of fishing while our lunch settles then play cricket later.'

'Sounds as though you've got the whole day planned out,' she quipped, summoning a smile because she didn't want him to see how uneasy she felt.

'I most certainly have! Entertaining that pair for a whole day requires precision planning.' He rolled his eyes. 'There's no knowing what they might get up to if we don't keep them busy!'

Heather laughed, although she was very aware that he seemed to be deliberately trying to avoid any mention of what had happened. Was Ross just surprised that she'd opened up to him at last or was there another reason why he was reluctant to talk about it?

The thought lingered even though Heather was kept busy playing with the children. They fished in the stream and filled a couple of jamjars with silver-scaled tiddlers then had a boisterous game of cricket which bore little relation to the noble sport.

Ross sat Grace on his shoulders and ran backwards and forwards, scoring runs, each time Heather managed to hit the ball. Grace loved every second and shouted with glee as she clutched hold of his hair. By the time the game ended and Ross had declared that Josh's and Luke's team had won the match, they were all worn out.

Ross groaned as he lifted Grace down from his shoulders and flexed his muscles. 'You'd think I'd be used to carrying people in my job but every bit of me is aching!'

'I don't suppose you normally go racing around, carrying the people you rescue,' Heather observed dryly.

'That's a point.' He grinned at her and Heather felt the nameless little fear that had been eating away at her disappear when she saw the warmth in his eyes. 'Maybe I'm not ready for the knacker's yard just yet after all.'

'I didn't say that,' she said cheekily, neatly sidestepping when he made a grab for her. 'Oh, you'll have to be quicker than that, Station Officer Tanner. Your age is definitely showing!'

'Is it, indeed?' He made another lunge and Heather turned and fled up the field. He was far too quick for her, of course, and caught up with her before she could reach the safety of the hut. Lifting her off the ground, he swung her over his shoulder in a classic fireman's lift and strode back towards the river.

'I think a ducking is called for, cheeky monkey.'

Heather was laughing so hard that she could hardly speak. 'Don't you dare, you horrible man!' She appealed to the children who were obviously taken aback by the sight of two grown-ups behaving so crazily. 'Don't let him duck me in the water, kids!'

'Maybe you should put Heather down, Uncle Ross,' Josh said uncertainly. 'Girls don't like getting all wet and dirty.'

'Mmm, I suppose you're right.' Ross bent and set her gently on her feet. He grinned at her and it was all Heather could do to stop herself leaning forward and kissing him when she saw the love in his eyes.

'Thank you,' she said demurely, even though she knew her own eyes were sending out just as fervent a message. She turned when Josh slipped his hand into hers. 'And thank you, my hero, for saving me from a ducking!'

'That's OK,' Josh declared. He looked up at her with solemn brown eyes. 'It's been lots of fun playing cricket and everything, but can we go home now? I want to see Mummy and tell her what we've done today.'

Heather bent and hugged him. 'That sounds like a really good idea to me, poppet. Let's pack everything back into the car and then Uncle Ross can take you to the hospital.'

'Sure you don't mind having your day cut short?' Ross said quietly as the children hurried away to collect the cricket equipment and their jars of tiddlers.

'Of course not. I've enjoyed every second of it and so have the children, but it's natural that they should want to see Kate.' She laid her hand on his arm. 'We can always plan another day out once Kate is out of hospital.'

'Yes, of course,' he agreed rather flatly, before he moved away.

Heather frowned as she watched him going over to the twins. Why did she have a horrible feeling that he hadn't really meant that? If Ross loved her then surely he saw her as a permanent part of his future? So why had he given her the impression that there might not be more days like this to look forward to?

The roads were much busier than when they'd set off that morning so it took them some time to get back. The children had quickly fallen asleep in the back of the car and they didn't wake up when Ross stopped outside Heather's flat. He turned off the engine and glanced in the rear-view mirror.

'They must be worn out by all that fresh air.'

'I know how they feel.' Heather smothered a yawn and heard him chuckle.

'Looks as though there might have been another sleeping beauty in the car if it had taken me any longer to get here.'

'It's been touch and go whether I could keep my eyes open for the last couple of miles,' she admitted. 'It just didn't seem fair to fall asleep and leave you to do all the hard work.'

'Oh, you shouldn't have worried about that. I'd have had the pleasure of waking you up when we got here. That would have more than made up for it.'

His voice seemed to have dropped to a gravelly rumble. Heather shivered when she felt a little curl of excitement spiral down into the pit of her stomach.

'I'm a heavy sleeper if I drop off during the day,' she explained huskily. 'You might have had a hard job to wake me.'

'I'd have managed. I know a foolproof method for waking sleeping beauties.' His smile was so unashamedly sensual that her heart bounced against her ribs as the feeling of excitement grew. 'Would you like me to demonstrate it?'

'I'm not sure there would be much point when I'm already awake,' she demurred.

'You could always *pretend* to be asleep. It's not hard. Just close your eyes and relax. I'll do the rest.'

Heather closed her eyes because the temptation was just too great to resist. She jumped when she felt a cool breath of air flow over her cheek.

'Wh-what are you doing?'

'Shh. You're supposed to be asleep. How can I demonstrate my technique if you don't take this seriously?'

Once again she felt a cool flow of air caressing her skin as he blew softly on her face. Heather sat quite still, her eyes tightly closed as she felt the breeze ripple across her forehead, her eyelids, the short, straight slope of her nose. She was holding her own breath as she waited for it to reach her mouth but, instead of continuing its downward journey, the breeze changed direction and she shivered when she felt a trickle of deliciously cool air encircling her ear.

'You're doing very well for a beginner,' Ross murmured. 'I'd say you were real princess material. I've always believed that only a genuine princess could remain sound asleep while her prince was crashing his way through the forest to wake her.'

'Maybe all those princesses in the fairy stories weren't really asleep. Maybe they were just pretending as well, because they knew how the story was supposed to end,' Heather suggested in a throaty whisper.

'Good point,' he agreed, then stopped talking because his mouth was far too busy with more important things.

Heather gasped when she felt the gentle current flow over the heated pulse that was beating at the base of her throat. It moved to the other pulse on the opposite side of her neck then suddenly swooped upwards. She groaned when she felt a puff of air play across her mouth a moment before it was replaced by the warm sensuality of Ross's lips.

Her own lips immediately parted and her heart sang when she felt the swift invasion of his tongue. She wrapped her arms around his neck and pulled him towards her so they could deepen the kiss. Her eyes might have been tightly shut but she was wide awake now and not the least bit sleepy. Never had she experienced a kiss of such intensity and passion, a kiss that was so full of emotion and yet so demanding. It was little wonder that she felt emotionally exhausted when Ross drew back and rested his forehead against hers.

'Wow! That was some kiss, princess.'

'Mmm, I have to say that your technique leaves very little to be desired. I am most definitely wide awake now!'

'Thank you. I appreciate the compliment.' He laughed as he brushed his mouth over her hair. 'And do you know what was the best thing about it?'

'What?'

'That we didn't have an audience this time.'

Heather gasped. 'I'd forgotten about the children!'

Ross chuckled. 'Me, too, but they're still asleep, otherwise we'd have been inundated with questions by now.'

Heather shot an anxious glance at the children but all three were fast asleep. It was a relief because she would have felt dreadful about them witnessing such a passionate embrace.

Heat ran through because she couldn't believe that she had forgotten about them being in the back of the car. It just proved how hard she found it to think clearly when Ross was around. She reached for the doorhandle, knowing that she needed some time on her own to think about what had happened that day. It had been a huge milestone in her life and she needed to consider all the implications.

'I'd better let you go. You don't want to be too late taking the boys in to see Kate.'

'No, although they'll only be allowed to stay a few minutes, I expect. Still, they'll be able to see their new little sister and they'll be thrilled about that.'

'Has she got a name yet?' Heather asked, knowing that she was delaying getting out of the car because she hated the thought of leaving him.

'I don't think Kate and Mike have decided on one. They've changed their minds so many times I haven't got a clue what the baby will end up being called. I never realised it was so difficult to choose a name for a child!'

'Wait until you try thinking up names for one of your own,' Heather warned him, then felt her heart seize up because there was a very real chance that child might be hers as well if things worked out. Frankly, it was too much to deal with that thought right then. She quickly got out of the car and opened the rear door to lift Grace out of the child seat.

'I'll fetch the basket,' Ross told her, going round to the boot. He followed her up the path and took the keys from her so he could unlock the door to save her having to wake Grace. Setting the basket on the hall floor, he turned to her.

'I'll phone you later, Heather. OK?'

'Yes, fine. And thanks for today, Ross. We both enjoyed it.'

'It was my pleasure,' he said huskily, bending to kiss her and drop a kiss on Grace's curls as well.

Heather was deeply touched by the way he had included Grace so naturally. She waited to wave him off then carried

Grace to the bedroom and quickly undressed her. The little girl didn't stir as Heather popped her into her cot. It was rather early to put her to bed but there didn't seem any point in waking her up.

Heather left the bedroom door ajar and went into the sitting-room and sank onto the sofa. She took a deep breath as she thought about everything that had happened that day, from her talk with her mother that morning to Ross's final kiss before he had left her. It was hard to believe that so much had changed in a few short hours.

She'd told Ross that she was falling in love with him and that had opened the way to a whole new life. There was still a remnant of the old fear lingering inside her but she would find a way to deal with it. She wanted a future with Ross and that far outweighed everything else.

The next few days were so hectic that Ross felt as though his feet never touched the ground. He stayed at Kate's so he could take the twins to school each morning before he went to work and collected them from their friend's house each evening after he had finished. Mike was spending all his time with Kate because it appeared that she had suffered a slight loss of memory. Some things were perfectly clear to her but others she had forgotten. However, the more time Mike spent with her, the more her condition improved.

Ross was very aware that he'd had little chance to speak to Heather since their trip to the country. He phoned her each night but the telephone was a poor substitute for actually seeing her. He called into the accident and emergency unit when he took the twins to see Kate on Tuesday evening but Heather was busy in Resus. He had to be content with another phone call later that evening, but the more time they spent apart the more his uncertainties grew. Was he doing the right thing by letting her fall in love with him?

Everything came to a head on Thursday afternoon in the worst possible way. Red Watch were halfway through their shift when a call came in to say there were two men trapped on board a boat that had sunk in the River Thames. They'd been restoring an old barge when the gas cylinder they'd been using had exploded. The barge had sunk in about six feet of water, trapping both men inside.

Ross was already running through the problems they might encounter as he climbed into the fire engine. According to the river police, the tide was coming in and the stretch of river where the barge had sunk was well known for its treacherous currents. He turned to Baz Russell.

'I want you to get kitted up in underwater gear as soon as we arrive. You, too, Charlie. We'll have to cut through the hull to get them out but it's not going to be easy with the tide rising.'

'It's a nice day for a swim, though,' Baz replied chirpily. He was always cheerful, which was one of the reasons why he was one of the most popular members of the crew.

'There's swimming and there again there's *swimming*,' Charlie replied glumly. 'Can't see why you're so pleased at the thought of wading around in all that mud.'

'Oh, I don't know. Look on the bright side. It will probably do wonders for our complexions,' Baz shot back. 'I was reading an article in my mum's magazine about the amount of money those film stars pay for mud treatments. We're going to get the same thing for free!'

'So long as you remember to wash it off before you get back in this engine,' Jack Marsh warned him. 'We don't want you two stinking the place out, do we, lads?'

Ross shook his head in amusement as the others added their own comments. 'You lot are worse than a bunch of kids.' He sobered as Jack slowed the engine as they approached their turning. 'OK. We're almost there so forget the jokes and mind what you're doing. We all know how treacherous it can be in the river.'

He jumped down from the cab and went to speak to the police officer who was co-ordinating the rescue. A camera crew from one of the television stations were also there but Ross shook his head when a reporter tried to interview him. There was no time to waste. The two men were still alive apparently, trapped in an air pocket, but it was imperative they were brought out before the tide reached its peak.

Ross quickly organised his men and accompanied them to the riverbank. Terry and Jack attached safety lines to the two crewmen who were going into the water and handed them the cutting gear they would need. Ross checked his watch.

'You've got twenty minutes until high tide so you're going to have to work fast.'

'No problemo,' Baz replied cheerfully. He pulled on his face mask then disappeared into the murky water, and Charlie swiftly followed.

'Keep a close eye on those safety lines,' Ross instructed. 'I don't want any problems.'

He waited anxiously, keeping a watchful eye on the time. The water was rising steadily so that within a short time the section of hull that had been visible had disappeared. There was a glow coming up through the water from the oxyacetylene torches the men were using, but he couldn't see either Baz or Charlie because it was too muddy. He breathed a sigh of relief when Charlie suddenly emerged with one of the men who'd been trapped.

'Get them out of there!' Ross instructed. He looked back at the water but there was no sign of Baz with the other man. 'Where are they?'

'The other chap was panicking a bit,' Charlie wheezed, dragging in air. 'Baz seemed to have things under control, though.'

'The line's loose,' Terry suddenly shouted. 'It's either snapped or Baz has unclipped it.'

'Go back down and see what's happening,' Ross instructed. He stripped off his jacket as Charlie slid into the water. 'And somebody fetch me the other set of diving apparatus!'

He changed into the wetsuit in record time and strapped the air tank to his back. The camera crew was filming what was happening but he ignored them as he got ready. Charlie resurfaced just as he was about to wade into the water.

'I can't see any sign of them!' the man said frantically. 'There's too much mud swilling around because of the tide.'

Ross quickly attached himself to a safety line and plunged into the river. He could feel the current tugging him away from the bank but managed to get a grip on the barge's handrail. He used it to haul himself down but there was no sign of Baz or the man he'd been trying to rescue.

Ross searched further afield, feeling the current carrying him out to the centre of the river, where it was most dangerous. He knew he shouldn't be taking such a risk but he was desperate to find Baz. His safety line suddenly went taut as it reached its limit but there was still no sign of the men. They had completely disappeared. He was exhausted from trying to fight the current and had to use the safety line to help him get back to shore where the crew hauled him out of the water.

'Alert the river police,' he said tonelessly, stripping off his oxygen mask. 'Tell them there are two men missing.'

They stayed on site until they were ordered to return to base. They all knew there was no possibility of the men being found alive by then but it was difficult to walk away. The silence on the return journey was in stark contrast to the jocularity when they'd set out.

Ross knew there would be an inquiry into what had happened so he went straight to his office to write his report. He kept going over and over what he had done, wondering if he should have gone himself instead of sending Baz.

He sighed because who could say that he wouldn't have been swept away? It was the risk they all lived with, day in and day out. None of them knew if today might be the day when their luck ran out and the thought suddenly crystallised every single one of the fears he'd had in the past few days.

It could be him who didn't return next time. Whilst he was willing to accept the dangers of his job, he wasn't prepared to let Heather suffer.

He got up and went to the window, and his heart felt like a

lead weight as he stared across the city skyline because he knew what he had to do. He had to end his relationship with Heather.

'Hey, Heather, take a look at this!'

Heather looked round when she heard Mel calling her. They were in the staffroom, taking a break while it was slack, and Mel had just switched on the television to watch the early evening news bulletin. Heather wandered over to see what was happening and gasped when she saw Ross on the television screen.

'That's Ross!' she exclaimed.

'Uh-huh. Seems a boat capsized in the river this afternoon and they had to send for the fire brigade. There were two men trapped on board, apparently.' Mel sighed. 'One of the firemen was swept away, along with the chap he was trying to rescue. They're assuming they both must have drowned.'

Heather sank onto a chair as her legs gave way. 'Y-you don't mean Ross, do you?'

'No! Ross was in charge of the rescue, which is why they were showing his picture.' Mel groaned when she saw Heather's white face. 'Sorry! I didn't mean to scare you. Me and my big mouth, eh?'

'It's OK.' She tried to smile but it was a relief when Trish popped her head round the door to tell Melanie there was someone in Reception asking to speak to her.

Heather leant her head against the back of the chair but her nerves were so tightly strung that it wasn't easy to calm down. The thought that Ross might have been the one to have been swept away by the river that afternoon terrified her. Surely she would be making a big mistake if she followed her heart and got even more deeply involved with him?

Picking up the remote control, she changed channels and found a different news bulletin. Once again there was a report of the incident and she made herself watch it from start to finish. She needed to watch it so that it would drive home the full enormity of what she was doing.

Ross appeared in almost every scene as he organised the

rescue attempt with a confidence and efficiency that couldn't
help but impress her. He was a true professional at his job,
calm under pressure, steadfast in a crisis and undeniably brave.
She loved him so much and couldn't bear the thought of anything happening to him but, as she sat there and watched, she
realised that she was willing to take that risk if it meant they
could be together.

Heather switched off the television and took a deep breath.
All of a sudden the situation was so simple that she couldn't
understand why she hadn't realised it before. Losing Stewart
had been a terrible tragedy but she'd never once wished that
she hadn't met him. They had loved one another and that love
had enriched her life and given her Grace.

She felt the same about Ross. She didn't regret falling in
love with him even though she'd tried to prevent it. Maybe
there were no guarantees about how long they would have together but she needed him. Her life would be meaningless without him.

A sudden smile curved her mouth. And when she saw him
next, she would tell him that.

Heather was just about to deal with a patient when she saw
Ross come into the A and E unit. She felt her heart flip over
with pleasure and quickly handed the patient's notes to Mel.

'Can you tell Mrs Davies I'll be with her in a few minutes,
please?'

'Will do,' Mel replied, grinning at her. 'I take it that Station
Officer Tanner isn't here on official business?'

Heather laughed. 'Not if *I've* got anything to do with it!'

She hurried across the waiting area, uncaring what anyone
thought as she reached up and kissed Ross on the cheek. She
was sorely tempted to blurt out her news right then and there
but just managed to hold back. She was glad she had when she
suddenly realised that Ross had made no attempt to return her
greeting.

'Is everything all right?' she asked uncertainly, drawing back.

'Not really.' He smiled rather grimly and Heather felt her stomach lurch in apprehension.

'It's not Kate, is it? She hasn't suffered a relapse?'

'Kate is fine. I just need to talk to you, Heather.'

Once again Heather felt a chill run through her when she heard how distant he sounded. She had no idea what was wrong but there was definitely something troubling him.

'I'll be finished here in about fifteen minutes,' she explained, trying desperately to stay calm. 'I could meet you in the coffee-shop.'

'Make it the bar across the road, the one with the tables outside. I would prefer not to have people watching us.'

'All right.' Heather put a detaining hand on his arm when he turned to leave. 'What is this all about, Ross? Can't you at least give me an idea?'

'Let's wait until later, Heather.'

He didn't add anything before he left. Heather made her way to the cubicle where her patient was waiting but it was difficult to concentrate as she examined Beryl Davies's leg. The woman had been bitten by her dog and there was extensive tissue damage to her calf, which would require more than a few stitches to sort it all out.

Heather phoned the plastic surgery reg, sighing when she was told that he was in Theatre and that it would be at least half an hour before he could see her patient. She hung up, knowing that she couldn't leave until she'd spoken to him. She wanted to know what was wrong with Ross and every extra minute she had to wait was pure torture. What *was* it that he wanted to tell her?

It was almost an hour later before she made it to the bar. Ross was sitting at a table in the corner and he stood up when she approached. There was a flatness about his tone that increased Heather's nervousness so that she found it difficult to answer when he asked her what she would like to drink.

'Just mineral water, please.'

She sat down while he went to the bar. Unfastening her jacket she tried to remain calm but her heart was hammering.

She didn't even wait for him to sit when he came back with a tall glass of fizzy water.

'What's going on, Ross? What do you want to talk to me about?'

'I've been trying to think of an easy way to say this, Heather but there isn't one, I'm afraid.'

He sat down and she felt her heart curl up when she saw the regret on his face. 'I've decided that we shouldn't see one another again. I'm sorry, but I really and truly believe it would be best if we ended this right now.'

CHAPTER THIRTEEN

Ross could see the shock on Heather's face and could have wept. He desperately didn't want to hurt her but he had no choice. How could he take the risk of ruining her life as it had been ruined once before? He knew he was doing the right thing—the *only* thing—but that didn't mean he felt good about it.

'End things…?' She stopped and swallowed. 'I'm sorry, Ross, but I don't understand. Why do you want to end our relationship if you love me?'

Ross had known she would ask that. He also knew that if he told her the truth she would find a way to dismiss his fears, and he couldn't allow himself to be swayed.

'I think I may have got a bit…well, carried away when I told you that, Heather. I've had time to think since then and I realise it was a mistake to tell you I was in love with you.'

It was simply a distortion of the truth but he knew which way she would interpret it. He ground his teeth when he saw the colour drain from her face.

'So what you're saying is that you don't love me and that's why you want to end our relationship?' She didn't wait for him to answer as she pushed back her chair. 'I'm sorry, Ross. I never meant to cause you any embarrassment. I appreciate you being so honest with me.'

'Heather, wait!' he implored. He caught hold of her hand as she stood up. 'I never meant this to happen. You understand that, don't you?'

'Yes, of course I do.'

She gently released herself and his heart ached when he saw the way she was struggling to maintain her control. He'd done this to her! He had made her open up her heart and had then rejected her. He would never forgive himself. It was only the thought of how much greater her suffering might be if they continued seeing one another and something happened to him that gave him the strength to sit there as she left the bar.

Ross finished his drink and ordered another. He rarely drank alcohol because he preferred to keep a clear head but he needed something to dull the ache that night. He'd sent Heather away and, whilst it had been the right thing to do, it hurt unbearably. Maybe Heather would meet someone else in time but he would never find anyone he could love as much as her. Heather was everything he had ever dreamed of and she could never be his.

Heather was filled with despair as she made her way home. She could scarcely believe what had happened. Ross didn't love her! He'd been mistaken about his feelings for her!

The words ran through her head in time to the thunder of the train as it sped through the Underground tunnels so that she felt sick by the time she reached her stop. She walked the rest of the way home, knowing that she would have to put on a brave face for Grace's sake. Wasn't this what she'd always feared, that she would have her heart broken again and that it would affect her precious daughter? But what she had never anticipated was that she could feel such despair because a relationship had ended. She felt every bit as bereft as she'd felt when Stewart had died!

Grace was eager to tell her about nursery school so Heather sat on the sofa while the little girl showed her the pictures she had drawn. She admired the squiggly stick figures and asked questions but it was as though her brain had split itself into two. One side was responding as normal whilst the other was weeping for her lost love.

Grace was blissfully unaware of her distraction and chattered on but it was a relief when Sandra announced that she was going out to dinner again that night. Heather knew that she would never have been able to fool her mother and the thought of having to explain what was wrong was more than she could bear. She needed to come to terms with what had happened before she could talk about it.

She went to bed as soon as Grace was settled and spent a sleepless night going over everything Ross had said to her. She found it difficult to believe that he had changed his mind because he'd seemed so sure of his feelings. She felt completely exhausted when it was time to get up for work and was glad that Grace and her mother were still asleep because she wouldn't have been able to hide her distress from them. Maybe she would be able to cope by the time she returned home.

Ben was in the staffroom when Heather arrived at work. It was the first time she'd seen him since the previous week because he'd been off sick. He grinned when she went into the room.

'Hi. Remember me?'

'Just about. How are you, anyway? You certainly look a lot better than you did the last time I saw you,' she replied as she hung her coat in a locker.

'I'm feeling marvellous. One hundred per cent fighting fit, and raring to go!'

Heather summoned a smile. 'Let's hope you still feel like that at the end of the day.'

'Oh, I shall.' Ben suddenly frowned. 'You don't look so good this morning, though, Heather. Is something wrong?'

'No, I'm fine.' She turned away when she felt tears welling into her eyes. Reaching into her coat pocket, she found a tissue and blew her nose. 'I didn't get much sleep last night.'

'I expect you were upset about what happened yesterday,' Ben said sympathetically as he picked up the morning paper. There was a report of the river rescue splashed all over the front page and Heather quickly averted her eyes when she saw the photo of Ross.

'It's a real tragedy, isn't it? It must have brought it home to you what a dangerous job Ross does.'

'It did,' she said stiltedly, trying to keep a grip on her emotions. How ironic that she should have managed to conquer her fears at last all to no avail.

'I'm not sure if I could do a job like that. It takes tremendous bravery to put your life at risk on a daily basis.' Ben sighed. 'Although the hardest thing, I imagine, is knowing what it could do to those you love.'

'What do you mean?' Heather queried.

'That it's one thing to accept the risk but something entirely different to know that you're putting your wife or girlfriend through hell every time you go to work.'

'Do you think so?' Heather said slowly, her mind racing. Had Ross been worried about hurting her if anything happened to him? Was that the real reason why he'd told her that he wanted to end their relationship? Maybe she was grasping at straws but it seemed to make a lot of sense.

'I don't just think so, I know it's true.' Ben shrugged when she looked at him. 'Just over a year ago I found out that I had cancer of the colon. It came as a complete shock because you don't expect something like that to happen when you're my age. The consultant I saw was pretty upbeat about my chances but he made it clear there was no guarantee the treatment would work.'

'I had no idea!' Heather exclaimed, forgetting her own problems for a moment.

'I prefer not to talk about it,' he explained. 'Anyway, at the time it happened I was going out with someone I was really keen on but I decided it wouldn't be right to continue seeing her when the future was so uncertain. I was trying to protect her in my own way, but she took it very badly and that is something I regret.'

'Didn't you explain why you'd decided to end your relationship?' Heather asked slowly, churning over everything Ben had said.

'No. She's a doctor, too, and I knew she would only try to convince me that we could get through it together.' He shrugged. 'In a nutshell, I wasn't prepared to run the risk of ruining her life so I told her that I'd met someone else.'

'It must have been hard for you, though.'

'It would have been worse if I'd had to watch her giving up

her career to look after me,' he said firmly. 'All right, so the treatment was a success but the cancer could come back. I thought it had, in fact, because of all the trouble I've had recently, but it turns out that I've had a particularly virulent stomach bug. But I'm not sorry I ended things with Holly because at least it means she's been able to get on with her life without having to constantly worry about me.'

Abby arrived at that point so Heather let the subject drop. It was clear that Ben didn't want the staff knowing about his problems and she could sympathise with him. It was a surprisingly quiet day, which meant that she had more time than she would have liked to think about what had happened. She couldn't shake off the feeling that there was a lesson to be learned from what Ben had told her. Had Ross ended their relationship because he'd wanted to avoid the risk of her getting hurt?

By the time her shift came to an end, Heather couldn't stand it any longer. She needed to speak to Ross and find out if her suspicions were correct. She left the hospital, hailed a taxi and asked the driver to take her to Hexton fire station. Maybe she was setting herself up for a great deal of disappointment but if there was a chance that she and Ross could work things out, she wasn't going to let it slip away!

Ross had spent the day with various high-ranking officials. The river police had phoned early that morning to say they'd recovered two bodies from the Thames. He had been asked to identify Baz Russell to spare Baz's widowed mother the ordeal. He'd agreed immediately because it had been the last thing he'd been able to do for his young colleague.

He was clearing away some papers at the end of his shift when he glanced out of the window and saw a taxi drawing up. He gasped in astonishment when he saw Heather getting out of the cab. He hurried downstairs and met her at the door, feeling his heart pounding when he saw how solemn she looked.

'Are you all right?'

'Fine. I just wanted a word with you, Ross.'

'I really cannot see what we have to talk about,' he said shortly, struggling to keep a grip on himself. Just seeing her again had thrown him completely off track. It was all he could do not to sweep her into his arms and tell her that he hadn't meant what he'd said, and that would be wrong. He had to think about Heather, not himself.

'I disagree. I think we have a lot to talk about, starting with the reason why you lied to me.'

There was a hint of defiance in her voice that made his heart kick up a storm when he heard it. 'You didn't make a mistake about your feelings, did you, Ross? You are in love with me. You can deny it all you like but we both know it's true. You love me every bit as much as I love you!'

'Heather, I... Oh, hell!' He groaned as he pulled her into his arms because he simply couldn't find the strength to lie to her again. 'Of course I love you!' he ground out between clenched teeth. 'I worship you, Heather, but that doesn't mean this is right!'

She drew back and looked steadily at him. 'Because you're afraid of breaking my heart if anything happens to you?'

She touched him lightly on the cheek and there was such love on her face that Ross's knees turned to water. 'But don't you know that you are going to break my heart if you send me away? I love you, Ross. I need you. I know there are no guarantees about how long we shall have together, but that just makes it more important that we don't waste a single second.'

'And you really and truly believe you could cope with the thought of me being in constant danger?' he said huskily, hardly daring to believe what he was hearing.

'I can cope with anything so long as I have you.'

Ross didn't know what to do because it was obvious that she was telling him the truth. He glanced round as one of the crew shouted goodnight to him. He could see the interest they were attracting and knew that they couldn't discuss this there. He handed Heather his car keys.

'Will you wait in the car while I finish clearing up?'

'Of course.' She smiled at him and he could feel warmth
envelop him because she'd made no attempt to hide her feelings.

Ross hurried back inside in a daze and handed over to the
officer in charge of Blue Watch. It took him barely five minutes
to change out of his uniform. Heather smiled when he opened
the car door.

'You were quick.'

'I didn't want to keep you waiting.' He started the engine
then glanced at her. 'Shall we go to my flat?'

'Yes, please. It's about time I saw where you live, don't you
think?'

There was a note of warm amusement in her voice that made
his skin prickle with anticipation. It was all he could do to keep
his mind on the road when it kept racing ahead to what would
happen when they reached his flat. Neither of them said a word
on the way there, as though they both sensed how superfluous
small-talk would be.

Ross parked the car then led the way up the stairs to the
third floor and unlocked his front door. Heather stepped inside
and looked around with obvious interest, but the last thing Ross
was concerned about was her opinion of his decor. He closed
the door with an impatient thud that made her turn to look at
him and what she must have seen on his face made her smile.

'Shall we talk now or later?' she murmured provocatively.

'Later,' he bit out, and reached for her. Their bodies collided
with a jolt and he groaned when he felt the firmness of her
breasts against his chest. All she had on was a thin cotton
blouse and he could feel the hardness of her nipples digging
into him. He cupped her breasts in his hands, stroking her nipples with the pads of his thumbs until she gasped. When he
started to unbutton her blouse she didn't protest but he could
feel her trembling.

The first button slid through its buttonhole then a second and
a third before he had to pause because his heart was beating
so fast that he felt quite dizzy. He pushed apart the collar of
her blouse and kissed her throat, the upper curve of her breasts,

the valley between them, and gained a little strength from the taste and feel of her, enough at least so that he could continue. The last button was finally undone and he pushed the blouse off her shoulders and let it slide down her arms. She was wearing a white lace bra and the sight of her pearly skin gleaming through the delicate net made him groan out loud.

'You are so beautiful, Heather. I know I should be sensible but I want to make love to you so much!'

'I want it, too, Ross.' She framed his face between her hands and looked at him. 'I love you. I want you. I know why you tried to split up and I love you all the more for caring so much about me. But I won't be truly happy unless we can be together.'

He pressed butterfly soft kisses over her parted lips. 'It's what I want more than anything but I couldn't bear to think what it could do to you if anything happened to me. You've suffered enough pain in your life, my darling.'

'Losing Stewart like that was dreadful,' she admitted honestly. 'It was even worse because I was pregnant and I felt so guilty about not having told him. But if I let you go because I'm afraid of what might happen then I would be giving up, and I know Stewart would hate that because he was always such a positive person.'

'Do you think you could ever come to love me as much as you loved him?' he asked shakily because she'd sounded so sure of herself.

'There will always be a special place in my heart for Stewart because he was Grace's father and I loved him, but my feelings for you, Ross, are very different. You make me feel things I've never felt for anyone before....'

Her voice tailed off as she stood on tiptoe and kissed him. Ross held her tightly, knowing how close he had come to losing her. He returned her kiss then swept her into his arms and carried her into the bedroom and laid her on the bed. He finished undressing her then quickly undressed himself and lay down beside her.

'I love you, Heather. I love you so much that it's hard to find the right words to tell you how I feel.'

'Then don't try.'

She slid her arms around his neck and pulled him down towards her. 'Just show me how you feel instead....'

Six months later...

'Heather, are you ready? We don't want to be late.'

Ross looked round as the door opened. His niece was being christened that day and he and Heather had been asked to stand as godparents for little Emma Louise. He whistled appreciatively when he saw how lovely Heather looked in the elegant pale blue suit she had chosen to wear for the occasion.

'Wow! I'm speechless.'

'You always were better with actions than words,' she teased, crossing the room to kiss him. She backed away when he went to draw her into his arms. 'I thought you said we were late?'

'Not *that* late.' He stole another kiss then sighed regretfully. 'I suppose I'd better behave myself or I'll spoil your lipstick.'

'You already have but I don't mind.' Heather turned to peer into the mirror. She carefully removed a smudge of lipstick from the corner of her mouth then straightened the lapels of her suit. 'You do realise that it's our anniversary today, don't you? We've been married for one whole month.'

'I know and it gets better every day.'

He slid his arms around her, kissing the nape of her neck and groaning as he felt his body immediately respond to her closeness. 'Feel what you do to me?'

'Mmm.' She smiled at him in the mirror. 'Are you sure we haven't got a few minutes to spare?'

'I wish we had but Kate will have my guts for garters if I'm late. I've had strict instructions that it's the duty of the god-parents to be on time.' He grinned wickedly. 'I think she had an idea we might get sidetracked, which is why she issued the warning. Still, I suppose I should be grateful that she's back to her normal, bossy self!'

'You should.' Heather laughed. 'Ah, well, I suppose we shall just have to wait until after the christening to have our celebration.'

'What celebration?' Ross demanded. 'Don't tell me your mother has decided to marry David. That will make it two weddings and a christening all in the space of a few months!'

'It's definitely on the cards but, no, that isn't the reason why we shall be celebrating tonight.' She turned and put her arms around him and he saw the excitement in her eyes. 'I'm pregnant, Ross.'

'Pregnant? But how…when…?' He stopped and gulped. 'Are you sure?'

'Yes.' She frowned. 'I know we weren't planning on having a baby just yet but you are pleased…?'

'Pleased? I'm thrilled! It's the most wonderful thing that could have happened!'

He swept her into his arms and spun her round. Heather laughed as she clung to him. 'You're making me dizzy!'

'Sorry.' He set her carefully down on her feet. 'When is the baby due?'

'In a little under eight months' time.' She smiled at him. 'I did a test as soon as I suspected I might be pregnant. I couldn't wait to tell you.'

'I'm so glad. It means we'll have even more time to look forward to the baby's arrival,' he said thickly, dropping a kiss on her lips.

They both looked round when Grace came running into the room. Ross picked her up, holding her close as he looked at Heather over the top of the child's head. 'I love you so much, Heather.'

'I love you, too,' she whispered, her heart in her eyes.

'And me,' Grace demanded.

Ross laughed as he kissed the little girl's cheek. 'You, too, poppet. Mummy and I love you very much.'

He put Grace down and took Heather into his arms again.

'Thank you for making all my dreams come true. I never knew it was possible to be this happy.'

'And thank you for making me see what I was missing out on,' she whispered. 'You really are my hero, Ross.'

Reaching up, she pressed a kiss to his mouth. Ross groaned as he drew her to him. Maybe they could spare a few minutes to celebrate....

Modern Romance™
...seduction and
passion guaranteed

Tender Romance™
...love affairs that
last a lifetime

Medical Romance™
...medical drama
on the pulse

Historical Romance™
...rich, vivid and
passionate

Sensual Romance™
...sassy, sexy and
seductive

Blaze Romance™
...the temperature's
rising

27 new titles every month.

Live the emotion

MILLS & BOON®

MB3

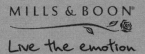

Medical Romance™

STORMBOUND SURGEON by *Marion Lennox*

Joss Braden is bored. In fact he's out of Iluka as fast as his sports car can take him! But the bridge is down – there's no way on or off the headland. Suddenly Joss is responsible for a whole town's health, with only Amy Freye's nursing home as a makeshift hospital – and the chemistry between Joss and Amy is incredible!

OUTBACK SURGEON by *Leah Martyn*

Gorgeous Nick Tonnelli isn't just a high-flying surgeon, he's also a Sydney socialite. Outback GP Abbey Jones is charmed but confused when he makes his interest clear. The attraction between them is overwhelming, but will the glamorous surgeon really want a relationship with her?

THE DOCTOR'S ENGAGEMENT WISH
by *Gill Sanderson*

Erin Hunter had been the most beautiful girl at school – and like all the boys Josh Harrison had been in love with her. Now they have been reunited, while working as GPs, and Josh finds his attraction to Erin as strong as ever. But Erin isn't as carefree as he remembers, and he is determined to discover what has changed her...

On sale 4th July 2003

Available at most branches of WH Smith, Tesco, Martins, Borders, Eason, Sainsbury's and all good paperback bookshops.

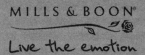

Live the emotion

... and get carried away with these three red-hot reads!

Miranda Lee
Caroline Anderson
Julia Byrne

MILLS & BOON

Available from 20th June 2003

*Available at most branches of WH Smith,
Tesco, Martins, Borders, Eason, Sainsbury's
and all good paperback bookshops.*

0703/024/MB77

FREE
4 BOOKS
AND A SURPRISE GIFT!

We would like to take this opportunity to thank you for reading this Mills & Boon® book by offering you the chance to take FOUR more specially selected titles from the Medical Romance™ series absolutely FREE! We're also making this offer to introduce you to the benefits of the Reader Service™—

★ FREE home delivery   ★ FREE gifts and competitions
★ FREE monthly Newsletter   ★ Exclusive Reader Service discount
★ Books available before they're in the shops

Accepting these FREE books and gift places you under no obligation to buy; you may cancel at any time, even after receiving your free shipment. Simply complete your details below and return the entire page to the address below. *You don't even need a stamp!*

YES! Please send me 4 free Medical Romance books and a surprise gift. I understand that unless you hear from me, I will receive 6 superb new titles every month for just £2.60 each, postage and packing free. I am under no obligation to purchase any books and may cancel my subscription at any time. The free books and gift will be mine to keep in any case.

M3ZED

Ms/Mrs/Miss/Mr ....Initials ....
BLOCK CAPITALS PLEASE

Surname ....

Address ....

....

....Postcode ....

Send this whole page to:
UK: FREEPOST CN81, Croydon, CR9 3WZ
EIRE: PO Box 4546, Kilcock, County Kildare (stamp required)